I D A

GERTRUDE STEIN

IdA

A NOVEL

VINTAGE BOOKS
A Division of Random House
New York

Library of Congress Cataloging in Publication Data

Stein, Gertrude, 1874-1946.
    Ida.

    I. Title.
[PZ3.S8194Id7]   [PS3537.T323]   813'.5'2   72-692
ISBN 0-394-71797-X

Manufactured in the United States of America

Vintage Books Edition, September 1972

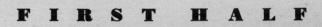

FIRST HALF

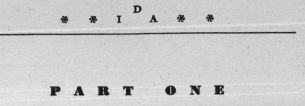

PART ONE

THERE WAS a baby born named Ida. Its mother held it with her hands to keep Ida from being born but when the time came Ida came. And as Ida came, with her came her twin, so there she was Ida-Ida.

The mother was sweet and gentle and so was the father. The whole family was sweet and gentle except the great-aunt. She was the only exception.

An old woman who was no relation and who had known the great-aunt when she was young was always telling that the great-aunt had had something happen to her oh many years ago, it was a soldier, and then the great-aunt had had little twins born to her and then she had quietly, the twins were dead then, born so, she had buried them under a pear tree and nobody knew.

Nobody believed the old woman perhaps it was true but nobody believed it, but all the family always looked at every pear tree and had a funny feeling.

The grandfather was sweet and gentle too. He liked

to say that in a little while a cherry tree does not look like a pear tree.

It was a nice family but they did easily lose each other.

So Ida was born and a very little while after her parents went off on a trip and never came back. That was the first funny thing that happened to Ida.

The days were long and there was nothing to do.

She saw the moon and she saw the sun and she saw the grass and she saw the streets.

The first time she saw anything it frightened her. She saw a little boy and when he waved to her she would not look his way.

She liked to talk and to sing songs and she liked to change places. Wherever she was she always liked to change places. Otherwise there was nothing to do all day. Of course she went to bed early but even so she always could say, what shall I do now, now what shall I do.

Some one told her to say no matter what the day is it always ends the same day, no matter what happens in the year the year always ends one day.

Ida was not idle but the days were always long even in winter and there was nothing to do.

Ida lived with her great-aunt not in the city but just outside.

She was very young and as she had nothing to do she walked as if she was tall as tall as any one. Once she was

lost that is to say a man followed her and that frightened her so that she was crying just as if she had been
lost. In a little while that is some time after it was a
comfort to her that this had happened to her.

She did not have anything to do and so she had time
to think about each day as it came. She was very careful
about Tuesday. She always just had to have Tuesday.
Tuesday was Tuesday to her.

They always had plenty to eat. Ida always hesitated
before eating. That was Ida.

One day it was not Tuesday, two people came to see
her great-aunt. They came in very carefully. They did
not come in together. First one came and then the other
one. One of them had some orange blossoms in her hand.
That made Ida feel funny. Who were they? She did not
know and she did not like to follow them in. A third one
came along, this one was a man and he had orange blossoms in his hat brim. He took off his hat and he said to
himself here I am, I wish to speak to myself. Here I am.
Then he went on into the house.

Ida remembered that an old woman had once told her
that she Ida would come to be so much older that not
anybody could be older, although, said the old woman,
there was one who was older.

Ida began to wonder if that was what was now happening to her. She wondered if she ought to go into the
house to see whether there was really any one with her
great-aunt, and then she thought she would act as if

she was not living there but was somebody just coming to visit and so she went up to the door and she asked herself is any one at home and when they that is she herself said to herself no there is nobody at home she decided not to go in.

That was just as well because orange blossoms were funny things to her great-aunt just as pear trees were funny things to Ida.

And so Ida went on growing older and then she was almost sixteen and a great many funny things happened to her. Her great-aunt went away so she lost her great-aunt who never really felt content since the orange blossoms had come to visit her. And now Ida lived with her grandfather. She had a dog, he was almost blind not from age but from having been born so and Ida called him Love, she liked to call him naturally she and he liked to come even without her calling him.

It was dark in the morning any morning but since her dog Love was blind it did not make any difference to him.

It is true he was born blind nice dogs often are. Though he was blind naturally she could always talk to him.

One day she said. Listen Love, but listen to everything and listen while I tell you something.

Yes Love she said to him, you have always had me and now you are going to have two, I am going to have a twin yes I am Love, I am tired of being just one and when I am a twin one of us can go out and one of us can stay in, yes Love yes I am yes I am going to have a twin. You know Love I am like that when I have to have it I have to have it. And I have to have a twin, yes Love.

The house that Ida lived in was a little on top of a hill, it was not a very pretty house but it was quite a nice one and there was a big field next to it and trees at either end of the field and a path at one side of it and not very many flowers ever because the trees and the grass took up so very much room but there was a good deal of space to fill with Ida and her dog Love and anybody could understand that she really did have to have a twin.

She began to sing about her twin and this is the way she sang.

Oh dear oh dear Love, that was her dog, if I had a twin well nobody would know which one I was and which one she was and so if anything happened nobody could tell anything and lots of things are going to happen and oh Love I felt it yes I know it I have a twin.

And then she said Love later on they will call me a suicide blonde because my twin will have dyed her hair. And then they will call me a murderess because there will come the time when I will have killed my twin which I first made come. If you make her can you kill her. Tell me Love my dog tell me and tell her.

Like everybody Ida had lived not everywhere but she had lived in quite a number of houses and in a good many hotels. It was always natural to live anywhere she lived and she soon forgot the other addresses. Anybody does.

There was nothing funny about Ida but funny things did happen to her.

Ida had never really met a man but she did have a plan.

That was while she was still living with her great-aunt. It was not near the water that is unless you call a little stream water or quite a way off a little lake water, and hills beyond it water. If you do not call all these things water then there where Ida was living was not at all near water but it was near a church.

It was March and very cold. Not in the church that was warm. Ida did not often go to church, she did not know anybody and if you do not know anybody you do not often go to church not to a church that is only open when something is going on.

And then she began to know a family of little aunts. There were five of them, they were nobody's aunts but they felt like aunts and Ida went to church with them. Somebody was going to preach. Was it about life or politics or love? It certainly was not about death, anyway, they asked Ida to go and they all went. It was crowded inside the church cold outside and hot inside. Ida was separated from the aunts, they were little and she could not see them, she was tall as tall as any one and so they could see her.

There was nothing funny about Ida but funny things did happen to her. There she was there was a crowd it was not very light, and she was close against so many, and then she stayed close against one or two, there might have been more room around her but she did not feel that way about it, anyway it was warm being so close to them and she did not know any of them, she did not see any of them, she looked far away, but she felt something, all right she felt something, and then the lecture or whatever it was was over.

She went out, everybody did, and soon she met the five little aunts, they did not seem to be liking her very much but they all went on together, it was cold it was in March and there was almost snow. There were trees of course there was a sidewalk but nobody was on it except themselves, and then all of a sudden some one a man of course jumped out from behind the trees and there was another with him. Ida said to the aunts go on go on quickly I will walk back of you to protect you, the aunts hurried on, Ida hurried a little less quickly, she turned toward the men but they were gone. The five aunts and Ida went on, they said good-night to her but she never saw them again. These were the first and last friends she ever had, and she really never went to church again not really.

When she got home her dog Love met her and she began to sing about her twin and this is the way she sang.

Oh dear oh dear Love (that was her dog), if I had a twin well nobody would know which one I was and which one she was and so if anything happened nobody could tell anything and lots of things are going to happen and oh Love I feel it yes I know I have a twin.

And then she began to look far away and she began to think about her parents. She remembered them when she grew a little older but there were plenty to take care of her and they did. (Think of all the refugees there are in the world just think.) And then one day she looked and she saw some one, she saw two of them but they were not her parents. She was learning to read and write then and the first thing she learned was that there were miracles and so she asked any one to give her one. Then one day, she said she had one. She sat alone and it was summer and suddenly it was snowing and as it snowed she saw two dogs a black and a white one both little and as she looked they both both the little dogs ran away and they ran away together. Ida said this was a miracle and it was.

Ida gradually was a little older and every time she was a little older some one else took care of her. She liked the change of address because in that way she never had to remember what her address was and she did not like having to remember. It was so easy to forget the last address and she really forgot to guess what the next address was.

Little by little she knew how to read and write and really she said and she was right it was not necessary for her to know anything else. And so quite gradually little by little she grew older.

She always had a dog, at every address she had a dog and the dog always had a name and once she had one and its name was Iris. Just at this time Ida was living up in the mountains. She liked it up there. But then Ida liked living anywhere. She had lived in so many places and she liked any where.

Her dog Iris was not afraid of thunder and lightning but he was afraid of the rain and when it began to rain he ran away from Ida and then he ran back to her because after all he could not run away from the rain because the rain followed him. And so he ran back again to Ida.

And then Ida left there and went to live in a city. She lived with her old grandfather. He was so old and weak you wondered how he could walk any farther but he always could. Ida paid no attention to her grandfather.

While she was in the city funny things happened to her.

It was the month of August. August is a month when if it is hot weather it is really very hot.

Some funny things happened then. Ida was out, she was always out or in, both being exciting.

She was out it was towards evening it was time when public parks were closed and Ida was looking in through the railing, and she saw right across the corner that some one else was looking and looking at her. It was a policeman. He was bending down and looking at her. She was not worrying but she did wonder why he was getting down to look at her across the corner. And then she saw

next to her a very old woman, well was it or was it not
a woman, she had so much clothing on and so many things
hanging from her and she was carrying so many things
she might have been anything.

Ida went away it was time for her to be at home.

Finally August was over and then it was September.

Sometimes in a public park she saw an old woman making over an old brown dress that is pieces of it to make
herself another dress. She had it all on all she owned in
the way of clothes and she was very busy. Ida never spoke
to her.

Ida was getting to be older. Sometimes she thought
about a husband but she knew that a husband meant
marriage and marriage meant changes and changes
meant names and after all she had so many changes but
she did have just that one name Ida and she liked it to
stay with her. And then another funny thing happened
to her.

It was winter and Ida never wondered because thunder rumbled in winter, that lightning struck and thunder
rumbled in winter. It just did.

Ida paid no attention to that but she did one day see
a man carrying an advertisement on his back, a sandwich
man, that was all right but what was funny was that he
stopped and he was talking as if he knew him to a big well
dressed rich man.

Ida very quickly went off home.

Then she went to live with another great-aunt outside of the city and there she decided and she told her dog Love about it, she decided that she would be a twin.

She had not yet decided to be a twin when another funny thing happened to her.

She was walking with her dog Love, they were walking and suddenly he left her to bark at something, that something was a man stretched out by the side of the road, not sleeping, because his legs were kicking, not dead, because he was rolling, not happy, because he just was not, and he was dressed in soldier's clothing. Love the dog went up to him, not to sniff, not to bark, he just went up to him and when Ida came near she saw he was not a white man, he was an Arab, and of course the dog Love did not bark at him. How could he when an Arab smells of herbs and fields and not of anything human? Ida was not frightened, he got up the Arab and he began to make motions of drinking. Ida might have been frightened if it had been toward evening, which it was, and she had been all alone, which she was, but she motioned back that she had nothing, and the Arab got up, and stood, and then suddenly, he went away. Ida instead of going on the way she was going went back the way she had come.

She heard about religion but she never really did happen to have any. One day, it was summer, she was in another place and she saw a lot of people under the

trees and she went too. They were there and some one
was moving around among them, they were all sitting
and kneeling, not all of them but most of them and in
the middle there was one slowly walking and her arms
were slowly moving and everybody was following and
some when their arms were started moving could not
stop their arms from going on moving. Ida stayed as
long as she could and then she went away. She always
stayed as long as she could.

One day, it was before or after she made up her mind
to be a twin, she joined a walking marathon. She kept
on moving, sleeping or walking, she kept on slowly moving. This was one of the funny things that happened to
her. Then she lived outside of a city, she was eighteen
then, she decided that she had had enough of only being
one and she told her dog Love that she was going to be
two she was going to be a twin. And this did then happen.

Ida often wrote letters to herself that is to say she
wrote to her twin.

Dear Ida my twin,

Here I am sitting not alone because I have dear
Love with me, and I speak to him and he speaks to
me, but here I am all alone and I am thinking of
you Ida my dear twin. Are you beautiful as beautiful as I am dear twin Ida, are you, and if you are
perhaps I am not. I can not go away Ida, I am here

always, if not here then somewhere, but just now I am here, I am like that, but you dear Ida you are not, you are not here, if you were I could not write to you. Do you know what I think Ida, I think that you could be a queen of beauty, one of the ones they elect when everybody has a vote. They are elected and they go everywhere and everybody looks at them and everybody sees them. Dear Ida oh dear Ida do do be one. Do not let them know you have any name but Ida and I know Ida will win, Ida Ida Ida,

> from your twin
> Ida

Ida sat silently looking at her dog Love and playing the piano softly until the light was dim. Ida went out first locking the door she went out and as she went out she knew she was a beauty and that they would all vote for her. First she had to find the place where they were going to vote, but that did not make any difference anywhere would do they would vote for her just anywhere, she was such a beauty.

As she went she saw a nicely dressed little girl with a broken arm who threw a stone at a window. It was the little girl's right arm that was broken. This was a sign.

So when Ida arrived they voted that she was a great beauty and the most beautiful and the completest beauty and she was for that year the winner of the beauty prize for all the world. Just like that. It did happen. Ida was her name and she had won.

Nobody knew anything about her except that she was Ida but that was enough because she was Ida the beauty Ida.

PART TWO

THERE WAS an older man who happened to go in where
they were voting. He did not know they were voting for
the prize beauty but once there he voted too. And naturally he voted for her. Anybody would. And so she won.
The only thing for her to do then was to go home which
she did. She had to go a long way round otherwise they
would have known where she lived of course she had to
give an address and she did, and she went there and
then she went back outside of the city where she was
living.

On the way, just at the end of the city she saw a
woman carrying a large bundle of wash. This woman
stopped and she was looking at a photograph, Ida
stopped too and it was astonishing, the woman was looking at the photograph, she had it in her hand, of Ida's
dog Love. This was astonishing.

Ida was so surprised she tried to snatch the photograph and just then an automobile came along, there
were two women in it, and the automobile stopped and

---

they stepped out to see what was happening. Ida snatched the photograph from the woman who was busy looking at the automobile and Ida jumped into the automobile and tried to start it, the two women jumped into the automobile threw Ida out and went on in the automobile with the photograph. Ida and the woman with the big bundle of wash were left there. The two of them stood and did not say a word.

Ida went away, she was a beauty, she had won the prize she was judged to be the most beautiful but she was bewildered and then she saw a package on the ground. One of the women in the automobile must have dropped it. Ida picked it up and then she went away.

So then Ida did everything an elected beauty does but every now and then she was lost.

One day she saw a man he looked as if he had just come off a farm and with him was a very little woman and behind him was an ordinary-sized woman. Ida wondered about them. One day she saw again the woman with a big bundle of wash. She was talking to a man, he was a young man. Ida came up near them. Just then an automobile with two women came past and in the automobile was Ida's dog Love, Ida was sure it was Love, of course it was Love and in its mouth it had a package, the same package Ida had picked up. There it all was and the woman with the bundle of wash and the young man and Ida, they all stood and looked and they did not any one of them say anything.

Ida went on living with her great-aunt, there where they lived just outside of the city, she and her dog Love and her piano. She did write letters very often to her twin Ida.

Dear Ida, she said.

Dear Ida,

So pleased so very pleased that you are winning, I might even call you Winnie because you are winning. You have won being a beautiful one the most beautiful one. One day I was walking with my dog Love and a man came up to him, held out his hand to him and said how do you do you the most beautiful one. I thought he was a very funny man and now they have decided that you are the one the most beautiful one. And one day the day you won, I saw a funny thing, I saw my dog Love belonging to some one. He did not belong to me he did belong to them. That made me feel very funny, but really it is not true he is here he belongs to me and you and now I will call you Winnie because you are winning everything and I am so happy that you are my twin.

Your twin, Ida-Ida

And so Winnie was coming to be known to be Winnie. Winnie Winnie is what they said when they saw her and they were beginning to see her.

They said it different ways. They said Winnie. And then they said Winnie.

She knew.

It is easy to make everybody say Winnie, yes Winnie. Sure I know Winnie. Everybody knows who Winnie is. It is not so easy, but there it is, everybody did begin to notice that Winnie is Winnie.

This quite excited Ida and she wrote more letters to Winnie.

Dear Winnie,

Everybody knows who you are, and I know who you are. Dear Winnie we are twins and your name is Winnie. Never again will I not be a twin,

Your twin

Ida

So many things happened to Winnie. Why not when everybody knew her name.

Once there were two people who met together. They said. What shall we do? So what did they do. They went to see Winnie. That is they went to look at Winnie.

When they looked at her they almost began to cry. One said. What if I did not look at her did not look at Winnie. And the other said. Well that is just the way I feel about it.

After a while they began to think that they had done it, that they had seen Winnie, that they had looked at her. It made them nervous because perhaps really had they.

One said to the other. Say have we and the other answered back, say have we.

Did you see her said one of them. Sure I saw her did you. Sure he said sure I saw her.

They went back to where they came from.

One day Ida went to buy some shoes. She liked to look at yellow shoes when she was going to buy red ones. She liked to look at black shoes when she was not going to buy any shoes at all.

It was crowded in the shoe store. It was the day before Easter.

There were a great many places but each one had some one, it is hard to try on shoes standing, hard, almost impossible and so she waited for her turn, a man was sitting next to his wife who was trying on shoes, he was not, and so not Ida but the saleswoman told him to get up, he did, and he did not look at Ida. Ida was used to that.

The place was full, nobody looked at Ida. Some of them were talking about Winnie. They said. But really, is Winnie so interesting? They just talked and talked about that.

So that is the way life went on.

There was Winnie.

Once in a while a man is a man and he comes from

Omaha, where they catch all they can. He almost caught Ida. It happened like this.

He went out one night and he saw Winnie. Winnie was always there. She went everywhere.

He followed Winnie.

He did it very well.

The next day he went and rang the bell.

He asked for Winnie.

Of course there was no Winnie.

That was not surprising and did not surprise him.

He could not ask for Ida because he did not know Ida. He almost asked for Ida. Well in a way he did ask for Ida.

Ida came.

Ida was not the same as Winnie. Not at all.

Ida and he, the man from Omaha said. How do you do. And then they said. Good-bye.

The Omaha man went away. He did follow Winnie again but he never rang the bell again. He knew better.

Ida lived alone. She tried to make her dog Iris notice birds but he never did. If he had she would have had more to do because she would have had to notice them too.

It is funny the kind of life Ida led but all the same it kept her going day after day.

But all the same something did happen.

One day she was there doing nothing and suddenly she felt very funny. She knew she had lost something. She looked everywhere and she could not find out what it was that she had lost but she knew she had lost something. All of a sudden she felt or rather she heard somebody call to her. She stopped, she really had not been walking but anyway she stopped and she turned and she heard them say, Ida is that you Ida. She saw somebody coming toward her. She had never seen them before. There were three of them, three women. But soon there was only one. That one came right along. It is funny isn't it. She said. Yes said Ida. There, said the woman, I told them I knew it was.

That was all that happened.

They all three went away.

Ida did not go on looking for what she had lost, she was too excited.

She remembered that one day in front of the house a man with a hat a cane and a bottle stopped. He put down the cane but then he did not know what to do with his hat, so he began again. He put his cane into a window so that stuck out, and he hung his hat on the cane and then with the bottle he stood up. This, he said, is a bottle and in it there is wine, and I who am drunk am going to drink this wine. He did.

And then he said.

It might be like having a handkerchief in a drawer and never taking it out but always knowing it was there. It would always be new and nobody ever would be through with having it there.

What is peace what is war said the man, what is beauty

what is ice, said the man. Where is my hat, said the man, where is my wine said the man, I have a cane, he said, I have a hat, he said, I have a bottle full of wine. Goodbye, he said, but Ida had gone away.

She had certain habits. When she counted ten she always counted them on her fingers to make ten times ten. It was very hard to remember how many times she had counted ten when once she had counted them because she had to remember twice and then when she had counted a hundred then what happened. Really nothing. Ida just sat down. Living alone as she did counting was an occupation.

She was walking and she saw a woman and three children, two little girls and a littler boy. The boy was carrying a black coat on his arms, a large one.

A woman said to Ida, I only like a white skin. If when I die I come back again and I find I have any other kind of skin then I will be sure that I was very wicked before.

This made Ida think about talking.

She commenced to talk. She liked to see people eat, in restaurants and wherever they eat, and she liked to talk. You can always talk with army officers. She did.

Army officers do not wear their uniforms in the cities, soldiers do but officers do not. This makes conversation with them easier and more difficult.

If an officer met Ida he said, how do you do and she answered very well I thank you. They were as polite as that.

He said to her. Thank you for answering me so pleasingly, and she said. You are very welcome.

The officer would then go on conversing.

What is it that you like better than anything else, he asked and she said. I like being where I am. Oh said he excitedly, and where are you. I am not here, she said, I am very careful about that. No I am not here, she said, it is very pleasant, she added and she turned slightly away, very pleasant indeed not to be here.

The officer smiled. I know he said I know what you mean. Winnie is your name and that is what you mean by your not being here.

She suddenly felt very faint. Her name was not Winnie it was Ida, there was no Winnie. She turned toward the officer and she said to him. I am afraid very much afraid that you are mistaken. And she went away very slowly. The officer looked after her but he did not follow her. Nobody could know in looking at him that he was an officer because he did not wear a uniform and he did not know whether she knew it or not.

Perhaps she did and perhaps she did not.

Every day after that Ida talked to some officer.

If I am an officer, said an officer to Ida, and I am an officer. I am an officer and I give orders. Would you, he said looking at Ida. Would you like to see me giving orders. Ida looked at him and did not answer. If I were to give orders and everybody obeyed me and they do, said the officer, would that impress you. Ida looked at him, she looked at him and the officer felt that she must like him, otherwise she would not look at him and so he said to her, you do like me or else you would not look at me. But Ida sighed. She said, yes and no. You see, said Ida, I do look at you but that is not enough. I look at you and you look at me but we neither of us say more than how do you do and very well I thank you, if we do then there is always the question. What is your name. And really, said Ida, if I knew your name I would not be interested in you, no, I would not, and if I do not know your name. I could not be interested, certainly I could not. Good-bye, said Ida, and she went away.

Ida not only said good-bye but she went away to live somewhere else.

Once upon a time way back there were always gates, gates that opened so that you could go in and then little by little there were no fences no walls anywhere. For a little time they had a gate even when there was no fence. It was there just to look elegant and it was nice to have a gate that would click even if there was no fence. By and by there was no gate.

Ida when she had a dog had often stood by a gate and she would hold the dog by the hand and in this way they would stand.

But that was long ago and Ida did not think of anything except now. Why indeed was she always alone if there could be anything to remember. Why indeed.

And so nothing happened to her yet. Not yet.

___

One day Ida saw a moth that was flying and it worried her. It was one of the very few things that ever worried Ida. She said to an officer. This was another officer. There is an army and there is a navy and there are always lots of officers. Ida said to this one. When you put your uniform away for the summer you are afraid of moths. Yes said the officer. I understand that, said Ida, and she slowly drifted away, very thoughtfully, because she knew of this. Alone and she was alone and she was afraid of moths and of mothballs. The two go together.

Ida rarely coughed. She had that kind of health.

In New England there are six states, Maine, Massachusetts, Vermont, New Hampshire, Connecticut and Rhode Island.

Ida turned up in Connecticut. She was living there quite naturally, quietly living there. She had a friend who was tall and thin and her eyes were gray and her hair was messed and she dressed in black and she was thin and her legs were long and she wore a large hat. She did not mind the sun but she did wear a wide-brimmed hat. Yes she did. She was like that. Yes she was.

This friend did not interest Ida. She saw her, yes, but she did not interest her.

Except this one woman nobody knew Ida in Connecticut. For a while she did not talk to anybody there. She spent the day sitting and then that was a day. On that day she heard somebody say something. They said who is Winnie. The next day Ida left Connecticut.

She began to think about what would happen if she were married.

As she was leaving Connecticut she began to listen to a man. He was an officer in the army. His name was Sam Hamlin. He was a lively Sam Hamlin. He said if he had a wife he could divorce her. He came originally from Connecticut and he was still in Connecticut. He said the only way to leave Connecticut was to go out of it. But he never would. If he had left Connecticut he might have gotten to Washington, perhaps to Utah and Idaho, and if he had he might have gotten lost. That is the way he felt about Connecticut.

Little by little very little by little he said it all to Ida. He said I know, and he said when I say I know I mean it is just like that. I like, he said to Ida, I like everything I say to be said out loud.

He said I know. He said I know you, and he not only said it to Ida but he said it to everybody, he knew Ida he said hell yes he knew Ida. He said one day to Ida it is so sweet to have soft music it is so sweet.

He told her how once upon a time he had been married and he said to her. Now listen. Once upon a time I was married, by the time you came to Connecticut I wasn't. Now you say you are leaving Connecticut. The only way to leave Connecticut is to go out, and I am not going out of Connecticut. Listen to me, he said, I am not going out of Connecticut. I am an officer in the army and of course perhaps they will send me out of Connecticut there is Massachusetts and Rhode Island and New Hampshire and Vermont and Maine but I am going to stay in Connecticut, believe it or not I am.

Ida left Connecticut and that was the first time Ida thought about getting married and it was the last time anybody said Winnie anywhere near her.

There was a woman in California her name was Eleanor Angel and she had a property and on that property she found gold and silver and she found platinum and radium. She did not find oil. She wrote to everybody about it and they were all excited, anybody would be, and they did believe it, and they said it was interesting if it was true and they were sure it was true.

Ida went out to stay with her.

Ida was never discouraged and she was always going out walking.

As she walked along, she thought about men and she thought about presidents. She thought about how some men are more presidents than other men when they happen to be born that way and she said to herself. Which one is mine. She knew that there must be one that could be hers one who would be a president. And so she sat down and was very satisfied to do nothing.

Sit down, somebody said to her, and she sat.

Well it was not that one. He sat too and then that was that.

Ida always looked again to see if it was that one or another one, the one she had seen or not, and sometimes it was not.

Then she would sit down not exactly to cry and not exactly to sit down but she did sit down and she felt very funny, she felt as if it was all being something and that was what always led her on.

Ida saw herself come, then she saw a man come, then she saw a man go away, then she saw herself go away.

And all the time well all the time she said something, she said nice little things, she said all right, she said I do.

Was she on a train or an automobile, an airplane or just walking.

Which was it.

Well she was on any of them and everywhere she was just talking. She was saying, yes yes I like to be sitting. Yes I like to be moving. Yes I have been here before. Yes it is very pleasant here. Yes I will come here again. Yes I do wish to have them meet, I meet them and they meet me and it is very nice.

Ida never sighed, she just rested. When she rested she turned a little and she said, yes dear. She said that very pleasantly.

This was all of Ida's life just then.

She said. I do not like birds.

She liked mechanical birds but not natural birds. Natural birds always sang.

She sat with her friend and they talked together. Ida said, I am never tired and I am never very fresh. I change all the time. I say to myself, Ida, and that startles me and then I sit still.

Her friend said, I will come again.

Do said Ida.

It was very quiet all day long but Ida was ready for that.

Ida married Frank Arthur.

Arthur had been born right in the middle of a big country.

He knew when he was a tiny boy that the earth was round so it was never a surprise to him. He knew that trees had green leaves and that there was snow when time for snow came and rain when time for rain came. He knew a lot.

When Arthur was little he knew a handsome boy who had a club-foot and was tall and thin and worked for a farmer.

The boy with the club-foot rode a bicycle and he would stand and lean on his bicycle and tell Arthur everything.

He told him all about dogs.

He told him how a little dog, once he had found out about it, would just go on making love to anything, the hind leg of a big dog, a leg of a table, anything, he told him how a young hunting dog's voice changed, it cracked just like boys' voices did and then it went up and down and then finally it settled down. He told him about shepherds' dogs, how shepherds only could work their dogs eight years that when the dog was nine years old the shepherd had to hang him, that often the shepherd was awfully sad and cried like anything when he had to hang his dog to kill him but he could not keep him after the dog was eight years old, they did not really care anything for sheep after that and how could you feed a dog if he did not care about sheep any more and so the shepherds sometimes cried a lot but when the dog was eight years old they did hang him. Then he told Arthur about another dog and a girl. She always used to give that dog a lump of sugar whenever she saw him. She was a girl in a store where they sold sugar, and then one day she saw the man come in who had the dog, and when he came she said where is the dog and he said the dog is dead. She had the piece of sugar in her hand and when he said that she put the piece of sugar in her mouth and ate it and then she burst out crying.

He told Arthur about sheep, he told him that sheep were curious about everything but mostly about dogs, they always were looking for a dog who looked like a sheep and sometimes they found one and when they did they the young ones the baby sheep were pleased, but the older ones were frightened, as soon as they saw a dog who really looked like a sheep, and they ran at him and tried to butt him.

He also told Arthur about cows, he said cows were not always willing, he said some cows hated everything. He also told him about bulls. He said bulls were not very interesting.

He used to stand, the boy with a club-foot, leaning on his bicycle and telling Arthur everything.

When Arthur was a little bigger he came to know a man, not a tall man. He was a fairly little man and he was a good climber. He could climb not only in and out of a window but out of the top of a door if the door was closed. He was very remarkable. Arthur asked him and he then heard him say that he never thought about anything else than climbing. Why should he when he could climb anything.

Arthur was not very good at climbing. All he could do was to listen to the little man. He told about how he climbed to the top of a gate, to the top of a door, to the top of a pole. The little man's name was Bernard. He said it was the same name as that of a saint. Then well naturally then he went away. He finally did go away alone.

Arthur was almost old enough to go away. Pretty soon he did go away.

He tried several ways of going away and finally he went away on a boat and got shipwrecked and had his ear frozen.

He liked that so much that he tried to get shipwrecked again but he never did. He tried it again and again, he tried it on every kind of boat but they never were wrecked again. Finally he said, Once and not again.

He did lots of things before he went back to the middle of the big country where he had been born.

Finally he became an officer in the army and he married Ida but before that he lived around.

One of the things he did was to sleep in a bed under a bridge. The bed was made of cardboard. He was not the first to make it. Somebody else made it but when Arthur had no place to go because he had used up all his money he used to go to sleep there. Some one always was asleep there. Day and night there was always somebody sleeping there. Arthur was one who when he woke up shaved and washed himself in the river, he always carried the things with him.

It was a nice time then. Instead of working or having his money Arthur just listened to anybody. It made him sleepy and he was never more than half awake and in his sleep he had a way of talking about sugar and cooking. He also used to talk about medicine glasses.

Arthur never fished in a river. He had slept too often under a bridge to care anything about going fishing. One evening he met a man who had been fishing. They talked a little and the man said that he was not much good at fishing, he saw the fish but he never could catch them. Finally he said to Arthur, do you know who I am. No said Arthur. Well said the man taking off his hat, I am chief of police. Well why can't you catch fish, said Arthur. Well I caught a trout the other day and he got away from me. Why didn't you take his number said Arthur. Because fish can't talk was the answer.

Arthur often wished on a star, he said star bright, star light, I wish I may I wish I might have the wish I wish tonight.

The wish was that he would be a king or rich.

There is no reason why a king should be rich or a rich man should be a king, no reason at all.

Arthur had not yet come to decide which one was the one for him. It was easy enough to be either the one or the other one. He just had to make up his mind, be rich or be a king and then it would just happen. Arthur knew that much.

Well anyway he went back to where he came from, he was in the middle of his country which was a big one and he commenced to cry. He was so nervous when he found himself crying that he lay full length on the ground turned on his stomach and dug his palms into the ground.

He decided to enter the army and he became an officer and some few years after he met Ida.

He met her on the road one day and he began to walk next to her and they managed to make their feet keep step. It was just like a walking marathon.

He began to talk. He said. All the world is crying crying about it all. They all want a king.

She looked at him and then she did not. Everybody might want a king but anybody did not want a queen.

It looks, said Arthur, as if it was sudden but really it took me some time, some months even a couple of years, to understand how everybody wants a king.

He said. Do you know the last time I was anywhere I was with my mother and everybody was good enough to tell me to come again. That was all long ago. Everybody was crying because I went away, but I was not crying. That is what makes anybody a king that everybody cries but he does not.

Philip was the kind that said everything out loud.

I knew her, he said and he said he knew Ida, hell he said, yes I know Ida. He said it to every one, he said it to her. He said he knew her.

Ida never saw Arthur again.

She just did not.

She went somewhere and there she just sat, she did not even have a dog, she did not have a town, she lived alone and just sat.

She went out once in a while, she listened to anybody talking about how they were waiting for a fall in prices.

She saw a sign up that said please pay the unemployed and a lot of people were gathered around and were looking.

It did not interest her. She was not unemployed. She just sat and she always had enough. Anybody could.

Somebody came and asked her where Arthur was. She said, Arthur was gone.

Pretty soon she was gone and when she was gone nobody knew what to say.

They did not know she was gone but she was.

They wanted to read about her but as there was nothing written about her they could not read about her. So they just waited.

Ida went to live with a cousin of her uncle.

He was an old man and he could gild picture frames so that they looked as if they had always had gold on them. He was a good man that old man and he had a son, he sometimes thought that he had two sons but anyway he had one and that one had a garage and he made a lot of money. He had a partner and they stole from one another. One day the son of the old man was so angry because the partner was most successful in getting the most that he up and shot him. They arrested him. They put him in jail. They condemned him to twenty years hard labor because the partner whom he had killed had a wife and three children. The man who killed the other one had no children that is to say his wife had one but it was not his. Anyway there it was. His mother spent all her time in church praying that her son's soul should be saved. The wife of their doctor said it was all the father and mother's fault, they had brought up their son always to think of money, always of money, had not they the old man and his wife got the cousin of the doctor's wife always to give them presents of course they had.

Ida did not stay there very long. She went to live with the cousin of the doctor's wife and there she walked every day and had her dog. The name of this dog was Claudine. Ida did not keep her. She gave her away.

She began to say to herself Ida dear Ida do you want to have two sisters or do you want to be one.

There were five sisters once and Ida might have been one.

Anybody likes to know about then and now, Ida was one and it is easy to have one sister and be a twin too and be a triplet three and be a quartet and four and be a quintuplet it is easy to have four but that just about does shut the door.

Ida began to be known.

As she walked along people began to be bewildered as they saw her and they did not call out to her but some did begin to notice her. Was she a twin well was she.

She went away again. Going away again was not monotonous although it seemed so. Ida ate no fruit. It was the end of the week and she had gone away and she did not come back there.

Pretty soon she said to herself Now listen to me, I am here and I know it, if I go away I will not like it because I am so used to my being here. I would not know what has happened, now just listen to me, she said to herself, listen to me, I am going to stop talking and I will.

Of course she had gone away and she was living with a friend.

How many of those who are yoked together have ever seen oxen.

This is what Ida said and she cried. Her eyes were full of tears and she waited and then she went over everything that had ever happened and in the middle of it she went to sleep.

When she awoke she was talking.

How do you do she said.

First she was alone and then soon everybody was standing listening. She did not talk to them.

Of course she did think about marrying. She had not married yet but she was going to marry.

She said if I was married I'd have children and if I had children then I'd be a mother and if I was a mother I'd tell them what to do.

She decided that she was not going to marry and was not going to have children and was not going to be a mother.

Ida decided that she was just going to talk to herself. Anybody could stand around and listen but as for her she was just going to talk to herself.

She no longer even needed a twin.

Somebody tried to interrupt her, he was an officer of course but how could he interrupt her if she was not talking to him but just talking to herself.

She said how do you do and people around answered her and said how do you do. The officer said how do you do, here I am, do you like peaches and grapes in winter, do you like chickens and bread and asparagus in summer. Ida did not answer, of course not.

It was funny the way Ida could go to sleep and the way she could cry and the way she could be alone and the way she could lie down and the way anybody knew what she did and what she did not do.

Ida thought she would go somewhere else but then she knew that she would look at everybody and everything and she knew it would not be interesting.

She was interesting.

She remembered everything and she remembered everybody but she never talked to any of them, she was always talking to herself.

She said to herself. How old are you, and that made her cry. Then she went to sleep and oh it was so hard not to cry. So hard.

So Ida decided to earn a living. She did not have to, she never had to but she decided to do it.

There are so many ways of earning a living and most of them are failures. She thought it was best to begin with one way which would be most easy to leave. So she tried photography and then she tried just talking.

It is wonderful how easy it is to earn a living that way. To be sure sometimes everybody thinks you are starving but you never are. Ida never starved.

Once she stayed a week in a hotel by herself. She said when she saw the man who ran it, how often do you have your hotel full. Quite often he answered. Well, said Ida,

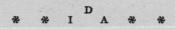
wait awhile and I will leave and then everybody will come, but while I am here nobody will come. Why not said the hotel keeper. Because said Ida, I want to be in the hotel all alone. I only want you and your wife and your three boys and your girl and your father and your mother and your sister in it while I am here. Nobody else. But do not worry, you will not have to keep the others out, they will not come while I am here.

Ida was right. The week she was there nobody came to eat or sleep in the hotel. It just did happen that way.

Ida was very much interested in the wife of the hotel keeper who was sweet-voiced and managed everything because Ida said that sooner or later she would kill herself, she would go out of a window, and the hotel would go to pieces.

Ida knew just what was going to happen. This did not bother her at all. Mostly before it happened she had gone away.

Once she was caught.

It was in a hilly country.

She knew two young men there, one painted in water colors and the other was an engineer. They were brothers. They did not look alike.

Ida sat down on a hillside. A brother was on each side of her.

The three sat together and nothing was said.

Then one brother said. I like to sit here where nothing is ever said. The other brother said. I I like bread, I like to sit here and eat bread. I like to sit here and look about me. I like to sit here and watch the trees grow. I like to sit here.

Ida said nothing. She did not hear what they said. Ida liked sitting. They all three did.

One brother said, It pleases me very much that I have discovered how prettily green looks next to blue and how water looks so well rushing down hill. I am going away for a little while. He said this to his brother. He got up and he went away.

His brother who was very polite did not go away as long as Ida stayed. He sat on and Ida sat on. They did not go to sleep but they almost stopped breathing. The brother said out loud. I am talking to myself. I am not disturbing any one. I feel it is better that everybody is dangerous than that they are not and if they are everybody will either die or be killed.

He waited a minute to listen to himself and then he went on.

I feel that it is easy to expect that we all wish to do good but do we. I know that I will follow any one who asks me to do anything. I myself am strong and I will help myself to anything I need.

Ida paid no attention.

Slowly this other brother went away.

Ida sat on. She said to herself. If a great many people were here and they all said hello Ida, I would not stand up, they would all stand up. If everybody offered me

everything I would not refuse anything because everything is mine without my asking for it or refusing it.

Ida understood what she was saying, she knew who she
was and she knew it was better that nobody came there.
If they did she would not be there, not just yet.

It is not easy to forget all that. Ida did not say that but
it is true it is not easy to forget all that.

It was very quiet all day long but Ida was ready for
that.

And then she went away.

She went away on a train in an automobile by airplane
and walking.

When she answered she looked around for water she
looked around for a bay, for a plowed field and then she
saw a man standing and she said to him, do you live here.
The man said no.

Ida was always ready to wait but there was nothing
to wait for here and she went away.

When she came to the next place she had better luck.
She saw two men standing and she said to them, do you
live here. They both said, they did. That did seem a
good place to begin and Ida began.

This time she did not talk to herself she talked to them.

She sat down and the two men sat down. Ida began.
She said. Do you know that I have just come. Yes said
one of the men because we have never seen you before.

The other man said, Perhaps you are not going to
stay.

I am not answered Ida.

Well then said one of the men it is not interesting and I am not listening.

Ida got very angry.

You are not listening to me, she said, you do not know what you are saying, if I talk you have to listen to what I say, there is nothing else you can do.

Then she added.

I never talk much anyway so if you like both of you can go away.

They both did go away.

Ida sat down. She was very satisfied to be sitting.

Sit again she said to some one and they sat, they just sat.

I do not think that Ida could like Benjamin Williams.

He did get up again and he did walk on.

Ida was not careful about whom she met, how could she be if she was always walking or sitting and she very often was.

She saw anybody who was on her way. That was her way. A nice way.

Ida went back again not to Connecticut but to New Hampshire. She sighed when she said New Hampshire.

New Hampshire, she said, is near Vermont and when did I say Vermont and New Hampshire.

Very often, she whispered, very often.

That was her answer.

This time she was married.

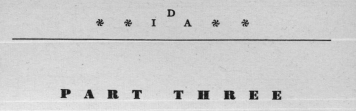
PART THREE

Ida did not get married so that never again would she be alone. As a matter of fact until the third time she was married she would not be married long. This first time she was married her husband came from Montana. He was the kind that when he was not alone he would look thoughtful. He was the kind that knew that in Montana there are mountains and that mountains have snow on them. He was not born in Montana. He had not lived very long in Montana, he would leave Montana, he had to to marry Ida and he was very thoughtful.

Ida, he said and then he sighed.

Oh Ida, he said.

How often, he said, how often have I said, Oh Ida.

He was careful. He began to count. He counted the number of times he said, Oh Ida.

It is not easy to count, said he to himself because when I count, I lose count.

Oh dear he said, it is lovely in Montana, there are

mountains in Montana and the mountains are very high and just then he looked up and he saw them and he decided, it was not very sudden, he decided he would never see Montana again and he never did.

He went away from Montana and he went to Virginia. There he saw trees and he was so pleased. He said I wonder if Ida has ever seen these trees. Of course she had. It was not she who was blind, it was her dog Iris.

Funnily enough even if Ida did see trees she always looked on the ground to see what had fallen from the trees. Leaves might and nuts and even feathers and flowers. Even water could fall from a tree. When it did well there was her umbrella. She had a very pretty short umbrella. She had lost two and now she had the third. Her husband said, Oh Ida.

Ida's husband did not love his father more than he did his mother or his mother more than he did his father.

Ida and he settled down together and one night she dreamed of a field of orchids, white orchids each on their stalk in a field. Such a pretty girl to have dreamed of white orchids each on its stalk in a field. That is what she dreamed.

And she dreamed that now she was married, she was not Ida she was Virginia. She dreamed that Virginia was her name and that she had been born in Wyoming not in Montana. She dreamed that she often longed for water. She dreamed that she said. When I close my eyes I see water and when I close my eyes I do see water.

What is water, said Virginia.

And then suddenly she said. Ida.

Ida was married and they went to live in Ohio. She did not love anybody in Ohio.

She liked apples. She was disappointed but she did not sigh. She got sunburned and she had a smile on her face. They asked her did she like it. She smiled gently and left it alone. When they asked her again she said not at all. Later on when they asked her did she like it she said. Perhaps only not yet.

Ida left Ohio.

As she left they asked her can you come again. Of course that is what she said, she said she could come again. Somebody called out, who is Ida, but she did not hear him, she did not know that they were asking about her, she really did not.

Ida did not go directly anywhere. She went all around the world. It did not take her long and everything she saw interested her.

She remembered all the countries there were but she did not count them.

First they asked her, how long before you have to go back to Washington.

Second they said, how soon after you get back to Washington will you go back to Ohio.

Thirdly they asked her. How do you go back to Washington from Ohio.

She always answered them.

She did not pay much attention to weather. She had that kind of money to spend that made it not make any difference about weather.

Ida had not been in love very much and if she were there she was.

Some said, Please like her.

They said regularly. Of course we like her.

Ida began to travel again.

She went from Washington to Wyoming, from Wyoming to Virginia and then she had a kind of feeling that she had never been in Washington although of course she had and she went there again.

She said she was going there just to see why they cry. That is what they do do there.

She knew just how far away one state is from another. She said to herself. Yes it is all whole.

And so there she was in Washington and her life was going to begin. She was not a twin.

Once upon a time a man had happened to begin walking. He lived in Alabama and walking made it seem awfully far away. While he was walking all of a sudden he saw a tree and on that tree was a bird and the bird had its mouth open. The bird said Ida, anyway it sounded like Ida, and the man, his name was Frederick, Frederick saw the bird and he heard him and he said, that kind of a bird is a mocking bird. Frederick went on walking and once every once in a while he saw another tree and he remembered that a bird had said Ida or something like Ida. That was happening in Alabama.

Frederick went into the army became an officer and came to Washington. There he fell in love with a woman, was she older was she younger or was she the same age. She was not older perhaps she was younger, very likely she was not the same age as his age.

Her name was not Ida.

Ida was in Washington.

If there are two little dogs little black dogs and one of them is a female and the other a male, the female does not look as foolish as the male, no not.

So Ida did not look foolish and neither she was.

She might have been foolish.

Saddest of all words are these, she might have been.

Ida felt very well.

PART FOUR

So IDA settled down in Washington. This is what happened every day.

Ida woke up. After a while she got up. Then she stood up. Then she ate something. After that she sat down.

That was Ida.

And Ida began her life in Washington. In a little while there were more of them there who sat down and stood up and leaned. Then they came in and went out. This made it useful to them and to Ida.

Ida said. I am not careful. I do not win him to come away. If he goes away I will not have him. Ida said I can count any one up to ten. When I count up to ten I stop counting. When she said that they listened to her. They were taken with her beginning counting and she counted from one to ten. Of course they listened to her.

Ida knew that. She knew that it is not easy to count while anybody listens to them, but it is easy to listen to them while they are counting.

More and more came to see Ida. Frederick came to see Ida.

Little by little Frederick fell in love with Ida. Ida did not stop him. He did not say that he was in love with her. He did not say that, not that.

And then he was and then they were all there together. He married her and she married him.

Then suddenly not at all suddenly, they were sent there, he was in the army, they got up and had decided to leave for Ohio. Yesterday or today they would leave for Ohio.

When they got to Ohio, Ohio is a state, it is only spelled with four letters. All of a sudden there they were in Ohio.

Ohio very likely was as large as that.

Everybody said to Ida and they said it to Frederick too. Smile at me please smile at me.

Ida smiled.

They settled down in Ohio.

What did they do in Ohio.

Well they did not stay there long.

They went to Texas.

There they really settled down.

It is easier for an officer in the army to settle down in Texas than in Ohio.

Ida said one day.

Is there anything strange in just walking along.

One day in Texas it was not an accident, believe it or not, a lizard did sit there. It was almost black all over and curled, with yellow under and over, hard to tell, it was so curled, but probably under.

Ida was not frightened, she thought she was thinking. She thought she heard everybody burst out crying and then heard everybody calling out, it is not Ohio, it is Texas, it is not Ohio.

Ida was funny that way, it was so important that all these things happened to her just when and how they did.

She settled down and she and Frederick stayed there until they were not there together or anywhere.

All this time Ida was very careful.

Everything that happened to her was not strange. All along it was not strange Ida was not strange.

It is so easy not to be a mother.

This too happened to Ida.

She never was a mother.

Not ever.

Her life in Ohio which turned out to be her life in Texas went on just like that. She was not a mother. She was not strange. She just knew that once upon a time there was a necessity to know that they would all leave Texas. They did not leave Texas all together but they all left Texas. She left Texas and he left Texas, he was Frederick, and they left Texas. They were all the people they knew when they were in Texas.

As they one and all left Texas, they all fastened their doors and as they fastened their doors nobody saw them leave. That is a way to leave.

Ida always left everywhere in some way. She left Texas in this way. So did they.

She left Texas never to return.

She never went back anywhere so why would she go back to Ohio and to Texas. She never did. Ida never did.

She did not go back to Frederick either.

Ida never did.

She did not remember just how many years she had been with Frederick and in Ohio and in Texas.

She did not remember even when she was with him and there because when she was there she did not count, that is she could count up to ten but it did not give her any pleasure to count then.

How pleasant it is to count one two three four five six seven, and then stop and then go on counting eight nine and then ten or eleven.

Ida just loved to do that but as she certainly was not in Ohio or in Texas that long and certainly not with Frederick that long counting was not anything to do.

Ida liked to be spoken to.

It happened quite often.

How do you do they said and she said it to them and they said it to her. How do you do.

Would you never rather be Ida, they said, never rather be Ida, she laughed, never, they said never rather be Ida.

Of course not, of course she would always rather be Ida and she was.

They all said everybody said, Never rather be Ida, it got to be a kind of a song.

Never, never rather be Ida, never rather be Ida.

Ida never heard anybody sing it. When she heard her name she never heard it. That was Ida.

And so it was all over that is Frederick was all over, Ida left Texas just as it was.

Before she left Texas she talked to Duncan. Old man Duncan they called him but he was quite young. He was forty-five and he had been a policeman and now he was a head of police and not in uniform, of course not, otherwise she would not have been talking to him.

He said to her, where were you before you came to Texas. He asked her that after they had shaken hands several times together and it was evening. It often was evening in Texas.

It is very easy to leave Texas, Ida said, not to Duncan, she just said it.

There is no harm in leaving Texas, no harm at all.

Ida said, I have not left Texas yet, but tell them, you and he, what are you, tell them that he has left Texas and tell them that you and he, well tell them about Texas, you and he.

So then suddenly, she was called away, they thought in Ohio, but she was called away to wherever she was. Just like that Ida was called away.

She was not there any more, because she was called away.

Duncan told her, that is he did not tell her because she was called away, but anyway he told her that he had not left Texas.

Duncan never did leave Texas except once when he went to Tennessee. But by that time he never wanted to leave Texas. No use saying that he only remembered Ida because he didn't.

Once upon a time there was a meadow and in this meadow was a tree and on this tree there were nuts. The nuts fell and then they plowed the ground and the nuts were plowed into the ground but they never grew out.

After Ida left Texas she did not live in the country, she lived in a city. She lived in Washington.

That is the way it went on. Washington is a city and a city well a city is well it is a city. Ida lived there.

Once upon a time every time Ida lived in a city she was careful, she really was. She might lose it lose being careful but really every time she lived in a city she was careful. She was careful in Washington. All who came in would say to her, well Ida how about it.

That is what did happen.

By the time it was all comfortable for Ida and everybody knew better, she knew just what would not be there for her. And it was not. It just was not there for her.

Just then somebody came in and he said here I am. He said to Ida if you were with me I would just say, say she is with me. By golly that is what we are like in Minnesota, Minnesota is just like that.

Hello Ida, said some one. And they said, No Ida we are not. Ida said, no I am not.

Ida felt that way about it. She said well sit down and cry, but nobody did, not just then.

So life began for Ida in Washington.

There were there Ida and two more, Ida kept saying to herself.

There whether there whether whether who is not.

That might have been the motto for Minnesota.

She did have to see those who came from Minnesota and hear them say, Minnesota is not old, believe it or not Minnesota is not old.

Ida began a daily life in Washington.

Once upon a time there was a shotgun and there were wooden guinea hens and they moved around electrically, electricity made them move around and as they moved around if you shot them their heads fell off them.

I thought I coughed said Ida and when I coughed I thought I coughed.

Ida said this and he listened to her he was not from Minnesota.

Once upon a time Ida stood all alone in the twilight. she was down in a field and leaning against a wall, her arms were folded and she looked very tall. Later she was walking up the road and she walked slowly.

She was not so young any more. It almost happened that she would be not sad not tired not depressed but just not so young any more.

She looked around her, she was not all alone because somebody passed by her and they said, it is a nicer evening than yesterday evening and she said, it was.

Ida married again. He was Andrew Hamilton and he came from Boston.

It is very usual of them when they come from Boston to be selfish, very usual, indeed. He and Ida sat together before they sat down.

But not, said some one seeing him, and who had heard of Ida, not, he said.

In Boston the earth is round. Believe it or not, in Boston the earth is round. But they were not in Boston, they were in Washington.

In Boston they hear the ocean as well. Not in Washington. There they have the river, the Potomac.

They were being married, it was not exciting, it was what they did. They did get married.

Once upon a time all who had anywhere to go did not go. This is what they did.

Ida was married again this time he came from Boston, she remembered his name. She was good friends with all her husbands.

This one came from Boston. They said Massachusetts, and when they said Massachusetts they remembered how fresh and green they were there, all of it, yes that is what they said.

In Washington it was different.

There it was in Washington it was come carefully and believe what they said.

Who is careful.

Well in a way Ida is.

She lives where she is not.

Not what.

Not careful.

Oh yes that is what they say.

Not careful.

Of course not.

Who is careful.

That is what they said.

And the answer was.

Ida said.

Oh yes, careful.

Oh yes, I can almost cry.

Ida never did.

Oh yes.

They all said oh yes.

And for three days I have not seen her.

That is what somebody did say somebody really somebody has said. For three days I have not seen her.

Nobody said Ida went away.

She was there Ida was.

So was her husband. So was everybody.

P A R T   F I V E

P O L I T I C S

THEY SAID, they do not want to buy from Ida. Why should they want to buy.

Ida and he.

He did not come from Louisiana, no. He was that kind. He did not only not come from Louisiana but he had had a carriage hound, a white and black spotted one and he the black and white spotted one was killed not killed but eaten by other dogs, they were all looking at a female dog and no one told him that the dog was nearly dead.

No one told him.

A young woman had silently had a way of giving the dog sugar and when she heard the dog was dead she ate the sugar.

And the man who was not from Louisiana added that, Oh yes he added that.

He and Ida.

He would have bought from Ida bought and well not well yes well no well why why not bought from Ida.

Ida was a friend.

She stayed in Washington.

She came to do what she knew each one of them wanted.

Easy enough in Washington.

She did not sell anything although they all wanted to buy.

Not at Bay Shore.

No not in Louisiana.

But in Carolina.

Not in North Carolina.

But in South Carolina.

Yes he would have bought from Ida in South Carolina but Ida was not there never there. She never was in either North or South Carolina. She was in Washington.

And so well yes so he did he did not buy from Ida.

Only Ida.

Well what did Ida do.

Ida knew just who was who.

She did. She did know.

They did not not an awful lot of them know Ida, just enough knew Ida to make Ida be just the one enough of them knew.

There are so many men.

What do you call them there.

There are so many men.

They did not all know Ida.

Now then.

In Washington, some one can do anything. Little by little it was Ida. She knew Charles and she smiled when she saw him. He wanted her to give him the rest of the morning. The rest of the morning. She was too busy too. She said, she never had anything to do but she did not give him the rest of the morning.

Woodward would not die of chagrin when he did not get what he had bought from Ida.

They all buy twice a day but the morning is the best time to buy. Woodward was a great buyer and he never did die of chagrin.

If he was no longer in Washington would Woodward die of chagrin.

Ida smiled every morning. She rested a good deal, she rested even in the evening.

Would Woodward come in and go out just as he liked.

Now that is a question a great question and Ida might answer, she might answer any question, but she did not find it as interesting as anything.

Would Woodward die of chagrin if he left Washington. Somebody stopped Ida and asked her this thing and she said nothing.

Then she said yes, Yes she said and she said nothing.

Yes they said yes would Woodward die of chagrin if he left Washington.

Almost at a loss Ida said yes, she did stand still and then she went on again.

Nobody ever followed Ida. What was the use of following Ida.

Ida had a dream. She dreamed that they were there and there was a little boy with them. Somebody had given the little boy a large package that had something in it and he went off to thank them. He never came back. They went to see why not. He was not there but there was a lady there and she was lying down and a large lion was there moving around. Where said they is the little boy, the lion ate him the lady said, and the package yes he ate it all, but the little boy came to thank you for it, yes I know but it did happen, I did not want it to happen but it did happen. I am very fond of the lion. They went away wondering and then Ida woke up.

Ida often met men and some of them hoped she would get something for them. She always did, not because she wanted them to have it but because she always did it when it was wanted.

Just when it was not at all likely Ida was lost, lost they said, oh yes lost, how lost, why just lost. Of course if she is lost. Yes of course she is lost.

Ida led a very easy life, that is she got up and sat up and went in and came out and rested and went to bed.

But some days she did rest a little more than on other days.

She did what she could for everybody.

Once in a while a father when he was young did not do it himself but a friend of his did. He took something.

When the policeman came nobody knew him. Most certainly he who later was a father refused to know him. They did not come from Africa, they came from North Carolina and Colorado. Later on the father had a son a young son and the young son began to go with men who stole. They were all then in Michigan so when they did steal they stole it again. The father was so worried, worried lest the police come and say to him your son is stealing, had he not refused when he was young and in North Carolina to recognize a friend who had stolen. He did say to the policeman then that he had never known that man although of course he had. And now, here in Michigan perhaps his own son was stealing. The policeman might come and how could he say he did not know his son. He might say it of course he might, he almost probably would.

Ida said to him I'll ask him. She meant that it was all right, it would be just like that, no trouble to anybody. Ida always did that. She saw the one who was all right and who would say yes yes it is all right and of course it was all right.

Ida did not need to be troubled, all she need do was to rest and she did rest. Just like that.

Once very often every day Ida went away. She could not go away really not, because she had no mother and she had no grandmother no sister and no aunt.

She dreamed that clothes were like Spanish ice-cream. She did not know why she dreamed of Spain. She was married in Washington, there was ice-cream there were clothes, but there was no Spain. Spain never came, but ice-cream and clothes clothes and ice-cream, food and clothes, politics, generals and admirals, clothes and food, she was married and she was in Washington.

She was not away from Washington.

No no more was there any day. She dreamed, if you are old you have nothing to eat, is that, she dreamed in her dream, is that money.

Ida had a companion named Christine. Christine had a little Chinese dog called William. Christine went away taking William. She thought of leaving him behind but she changed her mind.

When Christine went away she accomplished a great deal.

Oh Ida.

Ida was not married any more. She was very nice about it.

All around were what they found. At once they seemed all to like coming.

Ida did not leave Washington.

She rested.

Somebody said. Where is Ida.

Should she go away, somebody said. Go away like what.

Like what, they said.

Like Ida.

No said Christine and for this they thanked her.

All alone in Montana was a little man fragile but he smoked a pipe. Not then but later.

All alone there he was pale. Not tall. Not tall at all. All alone there he went about. He knew nobody was stout in Montana.

For this every little while he tried not to be thinner.

Dear Montana and how he went away.

It does not take long to leave Montana but it takes a long time to get stout, to put flesh on, get rosy and robust, get vaccinated, get everything.

In Montana he was never at a loss. Very likely not because he was careful of Montana.

He knew how to be careful and he was careful of Montana.

And so he plans everything.

He was a great success in Washington. Of course he was.

Politically speaking.

All of a sudden the snow had fallen the mountains were cold and he had left Montana.

That was when he began to smoke his pipe.

That was when he was a success in Washington.

That was when Christine had left him, naturally she had gone again. Now he knew Ida. Not to marry her. It was going to be quite a little while before Ida married again.

Ida moved around, to dance is to move around to move

around is to dance, and when Ida moved around she let her arms hang out easily in front of her just like that.

She kept on being in Washington.

Once upon a time, once very often a man was in Washington who was cautious. He came from Wisconsin although he had been born in Washington, Washington city not Washington state.

All right he liked it.

After a little while he was nervous again and then for them it was just as if he was cautious. How do you like it, they said. Then he said no. For that they were very willing that they could just as much as ever they could be used to it.

Oh believe me, he said, and then mountains, he said.

Of course there are no mountains in the city of Washington but there are monuments. Oh believe me, he said, there are mountains in Wisconsin. And everybody believed him.

Once when it happened to snow he stayed at home. I will, he said, I will stay at home and as I am at home I will think and as I am thinking I will say I am thinking. He did, he did stay at home, he did think and as he thought he did think that he would think. He did.

Gradually he wondered what it was he was thinking. He thought how very nice it is and then he said I can not help it.

Of course not of course he could not help it, dear Madison, dear Wisconsin.

He was born in the city of Washington but that just happened.

Ida was in Washington she was not thinking, all the time she was suffering because of his thinking and then he was not thinking about his thinking.

Dear Ida.

Ida very likely Ida was not only in Washington but most likely he would not forget to cry when he heard that Ida was never to leave Washington.

Never to leave Washington.

Of course she finally did.

But in the meantime Ida could not believe that it was best.

To be in Washington.

She knew only knew that she did not rest.

She did it all.

Ida did.

But enough, said some one.

And then Ida came in and sat down and she did rest.

When anybody needed Ida Ida was resting. That was all right that is the way Ida was needed.

Once upon a time there was a city, it was built of blocks and every block had a square in it and every square had a statue and every statue had a hat and every hat was off.

Where was Ida where was Ida.

She was there. She was in Washington and she said thank you very much, thank you very much indeed. Ida was in Washington.

Thank you very much.

While she was in Washington it was a long time.

There it was.

She was kind to politics while she was in Washington very kind. She told politics that it was very nice of them to have her be kind to them. And she was she was very kind.

She really did not get up in the morning. She wished that she could and they wished that she could but it was not at all necessary.

When she was up and she did see them she was kind.

She saw seven, or eight of them and she saw them one or perhaps two and each time it was a very long time. She never went away she always did stay.

This was what they did say.

How do you do, said Ida, how do you feel when I see you, said Ida, and she did say that and they liked it.

Of course they liked it. And then she was not tired but she did lie down in an easy-chair.

It was not really politics really that Ida knew. It was not politics it was favors, that is what Ida liked to do.

She knew she liked to do them.

Everybody knew she liked to do favors for them and wanting to do favors for everybody who wanted to have favors done for them it was quite natural that those who could do the favors did them when she asked them to do them.

It does go like that.

Once upon a time there was a man his name was Henry, Henry Henry was his name. He had told everybody that whatever name they called him by they just had to call him Henry. He came to Washington, he was born in San Francisco and he liked languages, he was not lazy but he did not like to earn a living. He knew that if anybody would come to know about him they would of course call him Henry. Ida did.

She was resting one day and somebody called, it was somebody who liked to call on Ida when she was resting. He might have wanted to marry her but he never did. He knew that everybody sooner or later would know who Ida was and so he brought Henry with him. Henry immediately asked her to do a favor for him, he wanted to go somewhere where he could talk languages and where he would have to do nothing else. Ida was resting. She smiled.

Pretty soon Henry had what he wanted, he never knew whether it was Ida, but he went to see Ida and he did not thank her but he smiled and she smiled and she was resting and he went away.

That was the way Ida was.

In Washington.

When it was a year Ida did not know how much time had passed. A year had passed. She was not married when a year had passed.

She was in Washington when a year had passed.

They asked her to stay with them and she did.

Once upon a time a man was named Eugene Thomas.
He was a nice man and not older than Ida. He was waiting
after he had been careful about coming in and going out
and everybody invited him. They said Eugene are you
married and he said perhaps he had been. He never had
been. That was the funny part of it he never had been
married. He liked to think that Ida had been married
and she had, of course she had been.

So that went on.

Ida was not tired, she went on staying in Washington.
Eugene Thomas pretty well stayed there too.

If a house has windows and any house has them anybody can stand at the window and look out.

He was funny Eugene Thomas, he used to say, There
is a treasure, That is a pleasure, It is a pleasure to her
and to him.

All these things did not really make Ida anxious to see
him. Ida was never anxious. Ida was tired. Once in a while
she knew all about something and when this happened
everybody stood still and Ida looked out of the window
and she was not so tired.

It is hard for Ida to remember what Ida said.

She said, I could remember anything I ever said. She
did say that.

Eugene Thomas was caught in a flood. And so he did
not marry Ida. The flood caught him and carried him
away. The flood was in Connecticut and he was so nearly
being drowned that he never came back to Washington.

But in the meanwhile Ida had begun to wonder, to wonder whether she had perhaps better begin to leave Washington and go elsewhere.

Not that she really went then, she was still resting. She saw a great many who lived in Washington and they looked at her when they saw her. Everybody knew it was Ida, not when they saw her, seeing her did not bring it home to them but hearing about her, hearing that she was Ida, it was that that made them know everything that Ida was to do. It was a pleasant Ida. Even when she was just tired with having besides everything had to come in after she had been out, it was a very pleasant Ida.

And so Ida was in Washington.

One day, it had happened again and again some one said something to her, they said Oh Ida, did you see me. Oh yes she said. Ida never did not see anybody, she always saw everybody and said she saw them. She made no changes about seeing then.

So he said to her Ida, your name is Ida isn't it, yes she said, and he said I thought your name was Ida, I thought you were Ida and I thought your name is Ida.

It is, she said.

They sat down.

She did not ask his name but of course he told her. He said his name was Gerald Seaton, and that he did not often care to walk about. He said that he was not too tall nor was he too stout, that he was not too fair and that he often had thought that it was very pleasant to live in

Washington. He had lived there but he thought of leaving. What did Ida think. She said she thought that very often it was very well to rest in the afternoon. He said of course, and then they did not leave, they sat there a little longer and they drank something and they thought they would eat something and pretty soon they thought that the afternoon was over which it was not.

How are you Ida said Gerald Seaton and she said, very well I thank you, and she said that they knew that.

Ida was not sure that she did want to marry not that Gerald Seaton had asked her, but then if Ida did want to marry well Gerald Seaton might go away and he might come back again and if while he was away she would want to marry and then when he was back again she still wanted to marry would she marry him.

They neither of them really said anything about any such thing. Gerald Seaton had not yet gone away and Ida had not yet wanted to marry, but but. Ida had friends, she stayed with them and they thought perhaps they thought that Ida would marry again perhaps marry Gerald Seaton.

Who is Gerald Seaton said the husband to his wife, who is any one said the wife to the husband and they liked to sit with Ida while Ida was resting.

Ida could always stay with a married couple, neither the husband nor the wife did not like to have her, they always wanted to make her life easy for her, it always was easy for her and they always wanted her to keep right on going to marry Gerald Seaton or whoever it was, now it was Gerald Seaton and he was going away. Nobody could say that he was not going away.

You see Edith and William are still talking about Ida as everybody is. Does it make any difference to Edith and William. Just enough so that like everybody they go on talking and they talk about Ida.

Edith and William were the married couple with whom Ida was staying.

They were not the ones who were anxious and ambitious, nor were they the ones who collected anything they were a quiet couple even though they were rich and they talked together.

Positively, said Edith, can you go on doing what you do do. Can you go on doing what you did do. This is what Edith told William she had said to Ida.

And William, laughed and then he broke into poetry.
At a glance
What a chance.
He looked at Edith and laughed and they laughed.
Edith went on being worried and William began again.
That she needs
What she has.
Edith said that William was foolish and Gerald Seaton was going away.

And they have what they are, said William.

Looking at William you never would have thought that he would talk poetry.

He liked to be in a garden.

Edith was worried not really worried but she liked to feel worried and she liked to look as if she felt worried, of course only about Ida.

Oh dear she said, and they have what they are said William chucking her under the chin.

Cheer up Edith he said let us talk about Ida.

And they like where they go

He murmured,

And Edith said Shut up.

Which is all after a while said William and then he and Edith said all right they would talk about Ida and Ida came in, not to rest, but to come in. They stopped it, stopped talking about her.

So Edith and William did not look at Ida, they started talking. What do you think said William what do you think if and when we decide anything what do you think it will be like. This is what William said and Edith looked out of the window. They were not in the same room with Ida but they might have been. Edith liked an opportunity to stand and so she looked out of the window. She half turned, she said to William, Did you say you said Ida. William then took to standing. This was it so they were standing. It is not natural that if anybody should be coming in that they would be standing. Ida did not come in, Edith went away from the window and William stood by the window and saw some one come in, it was not Gerald Seaton because he had gone away.

Let it be a lesson to her said Edith to William, but naturally William had said it first. Life went on very peacefully with Edith and William, it went on so that they were equally capable of seeing Ida all day every day, for which they might not feel it necessary to be careful that they shall after all realize what it is.

It is not early morning nor late in the evening it is just in between.

Edith and William had a mother but not living with them. She was waiting to come to see them but she was not coming any particular day. William had been married before and had a boy, Edith had been married before and had a girl, so naturally they did not have another one. It was very comfortable with them but Ida might go away.

It was a pleasant home, if a home has windows and any house has them anybody can stand at the window and look out.

Ida never did. She rested.

It was summer, it is pretty hot in Washington and Edith and William were going away to the country. Ida did not mind the heat and neither did Gerald Seaton. He was back in Washington.

How hot Washington is in summer and how much everybody in Washington feels the heat to be hot.

It was easy, Ida was Mrs. Gerald Seaton and they went away to stay.

It was a long time before they said all they had to say,

that is all Washington had to say about Ida and Gerald Seaton. But they were there naturally not since they were man and wife and had gone away.

This was not the only thing to do but they did it. They lived together as man and wife in other places. Which they were they were married, Ida was Mrs. Gerald Seaton and Seaton was Gerald Seaton and they both wore their wedding rings.

P A R T   S I X

THEY LIVED in a flat not too big not too small. And they lived there almost every day. They were not in Washington, they were far away from Washington, they were in Boston. There they lived almost as if Ida had not been Ida and Gerald Seaton had married any woman. They lived like this for quite a while. Some things did happen one of them was that they left Boston. Ida rested a good deal she liked to live in a smallish flat, she had never lived in a big one because she and Gerald could hear each other from one end of the place to the other and this was a pleasure because Ida liked to hear some one she liked to rest and Gerald Seaton did content her. Almost anything did content Ida although everybody was always talking about her.

Gerald Seaton did not look as if he had any ideas he was just a nice man but he did have some. He was always saying Ida knows a lot of people and if I have known them I have admired the ones I have known and if I have admired the ones I have known I have looked like them that is to say I do not look like them but they are like the ones I have known.

Ida did like to know that Gerald was in the house and she liked to hear him.

Gerald often said, I do not mean, I myself when I say I mean I mean, I do know how much I feel when once in a while I come in and I do. I am very busy, said Gerald and thinking does not take very much of my time, I do not think that is I do not feel that I do not like thinking.

All this would interest Ida also the way he would say I never think about Ida, everybody talks about Ida but I do not talk about Ida nor do I listen when they are all talking about Ida. I am thinking, Gerald would say, I am thinking of another person not any one whom I could possibly think would be at all like Ida not at all. This is what Gerald said and he did say that and that was the way it was.

Ida was not idle but she did not go in and out very much and she did not do anything and she rested and she liked Gerald to be there and to know he was talking.

So they went on living in their apartment but they did not live in Washington and later on they did not live in Boston.

If nobody knows you that does not argue you to be unknown, nobody knew Ida when they no longer lived in Boston but that did not mean that she was unknown.

She went away and she came again and nobody ever said they had enough of that.

What happened. She felt very well, she was not always well but she felt very well.

One day she saw him come, she knew he was there but besides that she saw him come. He came. He said, oh yes I do and she said thank you, they never met again.

Woodward George always worked, and he was always welcome. Ida said do come again. He came very often. When he came he came alone and when he came there were always at least a half dozen there and they all said, oh dear, I wish it was evening.

It almost looked as if Ida and Woodward would always meet, but Woodward went away and as they were not on the same continent, Ida was on one and Woodward was on another it looked as if they would not meet. But a continent can always be changed and so that is not why Ida and Woodward did not always meet.

Very likely Ida is not anxious nor is Woodward. Well said Ida, I have to have my life and Ida had her life and she has her life and she is having her life.

Oh dear said Ida and she was resting, she liked to get up when she was resting, and then rest again.

Woodward started in being a writer and then he became a dressmaker but not in Washington and not in Boston. Ida almost cried when she met his brother. She said what is your name and he answered Abraham George. Oh dear said Ida and she looked at him. Abraham George was a writer and he did not become a dressmaker like his brother and he and Ida talked together all the time. Abraham George even asked her questions, he said, you know I really think you are a very pleasant person to know, and Ida said of course, and she said I do like to do favors for anybody and he said do one for me, and she said what is it, and he said I want to change to being a widower and she said yes of course, and she did not really laugh but she did look very pleasant resting and waiting. Yes she did. After all it was Woodward George who was important to her but he was far far away.

She was still married to Gerald Seaton and houses came and houses went away, but you can never say that they were not together.

One day they went away again, this time quite far away, they went to another country and there they sat down. It was a small house, the place was called Bay Shore, it was a comfortable house to live in, they had friends among others she had a friend whose name was Lady Helen Button. How are you they said to each other. Ida learned to say it like that. How are you.

Ida liked it at Bay Shore. It did not belong to her but she well she did belong to it. How are you, she said when they came to see her.

A good many people did come to see her. Well of course she was married there was Gerald Seaton. How are you, was what they said to her, and they did sometimes forget to say it to Gerald but Gerald was nice and always said, oh yes, do, oh yes do.

She lived there and Gerald Seaton lived there, they

lived in the same apartment and they talked to each other when they were dining but not much when they were resting and each in their way was resting.

Ida knew a vacant house when she saw it but she did not look at it, would she be introduced to some one who did look at a vacant house. Never at any time did tears come to Ida's eyes.

Never.

Everybody knew that Andrew was one of two. He was so completely one of two that he was two. Andrew was his name and he was not tall, not tall at all.

And yet it did mean it when he came in or when he went out.

Ida had not known that she would be there when he came in and when he went out but she was.

Ida was.

Andrew, there were never tears in Andrew's voice or tears in his eyes, he might cry but that was an entirely different matter.

Ida knew that.

Slowly Ida knew everything about that. It was the first thing Ida had ever known really the first thing.

Ida somehow knew who Andrew was and leave it alone or not Ida saw him.

If he saw her or not it was not interesting. Andrew was not a man who ever noticed anything. Naturally not. They noticed him.

Feel like that do you said Ida.

Ida was busy resting.

Ida when she went out did not carry an umbrella. It had not rained enough not nearly enough and once a week Ida went walking and today was the once a week when she went walking.

Once a week is two days one following another and this was the second one and Ida was dreaming.

So much for Andrew.

There was hardly any beginning.

There never could be with Andrew when he was there there he was. Anybody could know that and Ida well she just did not know that and Andrew looked about him when she was there and he saw her.

She was married to Gerald and she and Gerald were just as old as ever but that did not bother them. They talked together at least some time every day and occasionally in the evening but that was all and when they talked she called out to him and he did not answer and he called out to her and mostly she did not answer but they were sometimes in their home together. Anyway they were married and had been for quite some time.

Andrew did not notice Ida but he saw her and he went away to meet some one who had been named after a saint, this one was named after a saint called Thomas and so his name was Thomas and so Andrew met Thomas that is to say Andrew went out to meet that is to say he would meet Thomas who was out walking not walking but reading as he was walking which was his habit.

Andrew was there and then Thomas came to him.

Everybody was silent and so were they and then everybody went away. Andrew went away first.

Ida went out walking later on and the rain came down but by that time Ida was at home reading, she was not walking any more. Each one reads in their way and Ida read in her way.

Andrew never read.

Of course not.

Ida was careless but not that way. She did read, and she never forgot to look up when she saw Andrew.

Ida went out walking instead of sitting in a garden which was just as well because in this way she often met everybody and stopped and talked with them, this might lead her to meet them again and if it did she sometimes met some one who cried for one reason or another. Ida did not mind anybody crying, why should she when she had a garden a house and a dog and when she was so often visiting. Very often they made four and no more.

This had nothing to do with Andrew who in a way was never out walking and if he was then of course nobody did meet him.

Andrew never disappeared, how could he when he was always there and Ida gradually was always there too. How do you do. That is what she said when she met him.

She did not really meet him, nobody did because he was there and they were there and nobody met him or he them, but Ida did, she met him.

Andrew, she called him, Andrew, not loudly, just Andrew and she did not call him she just said Andrew. Nobody had just said Andrew to Andrew.

Andrew never looked around when Ida called him but she really never called him. She did not see him but he was with him and she called Andrew just like that. That was what did impress him.

Ida liked it to be dark because if it was dark she could light a light. And if she lighted a light then she could see and if she saw she saw Andrew and she said to him. Here you are.

Andrew was there, and it was not very long, it was long but not very long before Ida often saw Andrew and Andrew saw her. He even came to see her. He came to see her whether she was there or whether she was not there.

Ida gradually was always there when he came and Andrew always came.

He came all the same.

Kindly consider that I am capable of deciding when and why I am coming. This is what Andrew said to Ida with some hesitation.

And now Ida was not only Ida she was Andrew's Ida and being Andrew's Ida Ida was more that Ida she was Ida itself.

For this there was a change, everybody changed, Ida even changed and even changed Andrew. Andrew had changed Ida to be more Ida and Ida changed Andrew to be less Andrew and they were both always together.

SECOND HALF

PART ONE

THE ROAD is awfully wide.
With the snow on either side.

She was walking along the road made wide with snow.
The moonlight was bright. She had a white dog and the
dog looked gray in the moonlight and on the snow. Oh
she said to herself that is what they mean when they say
in the night all cats are gray.

When there was no snow and no moonlight her dog had
always looked white at night.

When she turned her back on the moon the light suddenly was so bright it looked like another kind of light,
and if she could have been easily frightened it would have
frightened her but you get used to anything but really
she never did get used to this thing.

She said to herself what am I doing, I have my genius
and I am looking for my Andrew and she went on looking.

It was cold and when she went home the fire was out
and there was no more wood. There was a little girl serv-

ant, she knew that the servant had made a fire for herself
with all that wood and that her fire was going. She knew
it. She knocked at her door and walked in. The servant
was not there but the fire was. She was furious. She took
every bit of lighted wood and carried it into her room.
She sat down and looked at the fire and she knew she had
her genius and she might just as well go and look for her
Andrew. She went to bed then but she did not sleep very
well. She found out next day that Andrew came to town
every Sunday. She never saw him. Andrew was very good
looking like his name. Ida often said to herself she never
had met an Andrew and so she did not want to see him.
She liked to hear about him.

She would if it had not been so early in the morning
gone to be a nurse. As a nurse she might seek an Andrew
but to be a nurse you have to get up early in the morning.
You have to get up early in the morning to be a nun and
so although if she had been a nun she could have thought
every day about Andrew she never became a nun nor did
she become a nurse. She just stayed at home.

It is easy to stay at home not at night-time but in the
morning and even at noon and in the afternoon. At night-
time it is not so easy to stay at home.

For which reason, Andrew's name changed to Ida and
eight changed to four and sixteen changed to twenty-
five and they all sat down.

For which all day she sat down. As I said she had that
habit the habit of sitting down and only once every day

she went out walking and she always talked about that. That made Ida listen. She knew how to listen.

This is what she said.

She did not say Ida knew how to listen but she talked as if she knew that Ida knew how to listen.

Every day she talked the same way and every day she took a walk and every day Ida was there and every day she talked about his walk, and every day Ida did listen while she talked about his walk. It can be very pleasant to walk every day and to talk about the walk and every day and it can be very pleasant to listen every day to him talk about his every-day walk.

You see there was he it came to be Andrew again and it was Ida.

If there was a war or anything Andrew could still take a walk every day and talk about the walk he had taken that day.

For which it made gradually that it was not so important that Ida was Ida.

It could and did happen that it was not so important.

Would Ida fly, well not alone and certainly it was better not to fly than fly alone. Ida came to walking, she had never thought she would just walk but she did and this time she did not walk alone she walked with Susan Little.

For this they did not sing.

Such things can happen, Ida did not have to be told about it nor did she have to tell about it.

There was no Andrew.

Andrew stayed at home and waited for her, and Ida came. This can happen, Andrew could walk and come to see Ida and tell her what he did while he was walking and later Ida could walk and come back and not tell Andrew that she had been walking. Andrew could not have listened to Ida walking. Andrew walked not Ida. It is perhaps best so.

Anybody can go away, anybody can take walks and anybody can meet somebody new. Anybody can like to say how do you do to somebody they never saw before and yet it did not matter. Ida never did, she always walked with some one as if they had walked together any day. That really made Ida so pleasant that nobody ever did stay away.

And then they all disappeared, not really disappeared but nobody talked about them any more.

So it was all to do over again, Ida had Andrew that is she had that he walked every day, nobody talked about him any more but he had not disappeared, and he talked about his walk and he walked every day.

So Ida was left alone, and she began to sit again.

And sitting she thought about her life with dogs and this was it.

The first dog I ever remember seeing, I had seen cats before and I must have seen dogs but the first dog I ever remember seeing was a large puppy in the garden. Nobody knew where he came from so we called him Prince.

It was a very nice garden but he was a dog and he grew
very big. I do not remember what he ate but he must have
eaten a lot because he grew so big. I do not remember
playing with him very much. He was very nice but that
was all, like tables and chairs are nice. That was all. Then
there were a lot of dogs but none of them interesting.
Then there was a little dog, a black and tan and he hung
himself on a string when somebody left him. He had not
been so interesting but the way he died made him very
interesting. I do not know what he had as a name.

Then for a long time there were no dogs none that I
ever noticed. I heard people say they had dogs but if I
saw them I did not notice them and I heard people say
their dog had died but I did not notice anything about it
and then there was a dog, I do not know where he came
from or where he went but he was a dog.

It was not yet summer but there was sun and there
were wooden steps and I was sitting on them, and I was
just doing nothing and a brown dog came and sat down
too. I petted him, he liked petting and he put his head
on my lap and we both went on sitting. This happened
every afternoon for a week and then he never came. I do
not know where he came from or where he went or if he
had a name but I knew he was brown, he was a water dog
a fairly big one and I never did forget him.

And then for some time there was no dog and then there
were lots of them but other people had them.

A dog has to have a name and he has to look at you. Sometimes it is kind of bothering to have them look at you.

Any dog is new.

The dogs I knew then which were not mine were mostly very fine. There was a Pekinese named Sandy, he was a very large one, Pekineses should be tiny but he was a big one like a small lion but he was all Pekinese, I suppose anywhere there can be giants, and he was a giant Pekinese.

Sandy was his name because he was that color, the color of sand. He should have been carried around, Pekinese mostly are but he was almost too heavy to carry. I liked Sandy. When he stood up on a table all ruffled up and his tail all ruffled up he did look like a lion, a very little lion, but a fierce one.

He did not like climbing the mountains, they were not real mountains, they were made of a man on two chairs and Sandy was supposed to climb him as if he were climbing a mountain. Sandy thought this was disgusting and he was right. No use calling a thing like that climbing the mountains, and if it has been really mountains of course Sandy would not have been there. Sandy liked things flat, tables, floors, and paths. He liked waddling along as he pleased. No mountains, no climbing, no automobiles, he was killed by one. Sandy knew what he liked, flat things and sugar, sugar was flat too, and Sandy never was interested in anything else and then one day an automobile went over him, poor Sandy and that was the end of Sandy.

So one changed to two and two changed to five and the next dog was also not a big one, his name was Lillieman and he was black and a French bull and not welcome. He was that kind of a dog he just was not welcome.

When he came he was not welcome and he came very often. He was good-looking, he was not old, he did finally die and was buried under a white lilac tree in a garden but he just was not welcome.

He had his little ways, he always wanted to see something that was just too high or too low for him to reach and so everything was sure to get broken. He did not break it but it did just get broken. Nobody could blame him but of course he was not welcome.

Before he died and was buried under the white lilac tree, he met another black dog called Dick. Dick was a French poodle and Lillieman was a French bull and they were both black but they did not interest each other. As much as possible they never knew the other one was there. Sometimes when they bumped each other no one heard the other one bark it was hard to not notice the other one. But they did. Days at a time sometimes they did.

Dick was the first poodle I ever knew and he was always welcome, round roly-poly and old and gray and lively and pleasant, he was always welcome.

He had only one fault. He stole eggs, he could indeed steal a whole basket of them and then break them and eat them, the cook would hit him with a broom when she caught him but nothing could stop him, when he saw a basket of eggs he had to steal them and break them and eat them. He only liked eggs raw, he never stole cooked eggs, whether he liked breaking them, or the looks of them or just, well anyway it was the only fault he had. Perhaps because he was a black dog and eggs are white and then yellow, well anyway he could steal a whole basket of them and break them and eat them, not the shells of course just the egg.

So this was Dick the poodle very playful very lively old but full of energy and he and Lillieman the French bull could be on the same lawn together and not notice each other, there was no connection between them, they just ignored each other. The bull Lillieman died first and was buried under the white lilac, Dick the poodle went on running around making love to distant dogs, sometimes a half day's run away and running after sticks and stones, he was fourteen years old and very lively and then one day he heard of a dog far away and he felt he could love her, off he went to see her and he never came back again, he was run over, on the way there, he never got there he never came back and alas poor Dick he was never buried anywhere.

Dogs are dogs, you sometimes think that they are not but they are. And they always are here there and everywhere.

There were so many dogs and I knew some of them I

knew some better than others, and sometimes I did not
know whether I wanted to meet another one or not.

There was one who was named Mary Rose, and she
had two children, the first one was an awful one. This was
the way it happened.

They say dogs are brave but really they are frightened
of a great many things about as many things as frighten
children.

Mary Rose had no reason to be frightened because she
was always well and she never thought about being lost,
most dogs do and it frightens them awfully but Mary
Rose did get lost all the same not really lost but for a day
and a night too. Nobody really knew what happened.

She came home and she was dirty, she who was always
so clean and she had lost her collar and she always loved
her collar and she dragged herself along she who always
walked along so tidily. She was a fox-terrier with smooth
white hair, and pretty black marks. A little boy brought
back her collar and then pretty soon Chocolate came, it
was her only puppy and he was a monster, they called him
Chocolate because he looked like a chocolate cake or a
bar of chocolate or chocolate candy, and he was awful.
Nobody meant it but he was run over, it was sad and
Mary Rose had been fond of him. Later she had a real
daughter Blanchette who looked just like her, but Mary
Rose never cared about her. Blanchette was too like her,
she was not at all interesting and besides Mary Rose
knew that Blanchette would live longer and never have a

daughter and she was right. Mary Rose died in the country, Blanchette lived in the city and never had a daughter and was never lost and never had any worries and gradually grew very ugly but she never suspected it and nobody told her so and it was no trouble to her.

Mary Rose loved only once, lots of dogs do they love only once or twice, Mary Rose was not a loving dog, but she was a tempting dog, she loved to tempt other dogs to do what they should not. She never did what she should not but they did when she showed them where it was.

Little things happen like that, but she had to do something then when she had lost the only dog she loved who was her own son and who was called Chocolate. After that she just was like that.

I can just see her tempting Polybe in the soft moonlight to do what was not right.

Dogs should smell but not eat, if they eat dirt that means they are naughty or they have worms, Mary Rose was never naughty and she never had worms but Polybe, well Polybe was not neglected but he was not understood. He never was understood. I suppose he died but I never knew. Anyway he had his duty to do and he never did it, not because he did not want to do his duty but because he never knew what his duty was.

That was what Polybe was.

He liked moonlight because it was warmer than darkness but he never noticed the moon. His father and his sister danced on the hillside in the moonlight but Polybe

had left home so young that he never knew how to dance
in it but he did like the moonlight because it was warmer
than the dark.

Polybe was not a small dog he was a hound and he had
stripes red and black like only a zebra's stripes are white
and black but Polybe's stripes were as regular as that
and his front legs were long, all his family could kill a
rabbit with a blow of their front paw, that is really why
they danced in the moonlight, they thought they were
chasing rabbits, any shadow was a rabbit to them and
there are lots of shadows on a hillside in the summer
under a bright moon.

Poor Polybe he never really knew anything, the
shepherds said that he chased sheep, perhaps he did
thinking they were rabbits, he might have made a mistake
like that, he easily might. Another little little dog was so
foolish once he always thought that any table leg was
his mother, and would suck away at it as if it was his
mother. Polybe was not as foolish as that but he almost
was, anyway Mary Rose could always lead him astray,
perhaps she whispered to him that sheep were rabbits.
She might have.

And then Mary Rose went far away. Polybe stayed
where he was and did not remember any one. He never
did. That was Polybe.

And he went away tied to a string and he never did try
to come back. Back meant nothing to him. A day was

never a day to Polybe. He never barked, he had nothing
to say.

Polybe is still some place today, nothing could ever
happen to him to kill him or to change anything in any
way.

The next dog was bigger than any other dog had been.

When a dog is really big he is very naturally thin,
and when he is big and thin when he moves he does not
seem to be moving. There were two of them one was probably dead before I saw the second one. I did not know the
first one but I heard what he could do I saw him of course
but when I saw him he came along but he was hardly
moving.

It did not take much moving to come along as fast as
we were going. There was no other dog there which was
lucky because they said that when he saw another dog
well he did not move much but he killed him, he always
killed any dog he saw although he hardly moved at all to
kill him. I saw this dog quite a few times but there was
never any other dog anywhere near. I was glad.

The other one well he looked gentle enough and he
hardly moved at all and he was very big and he looked
thin although he really was not.

He used to walk about very gently almost not at all he
was so tall and he moved his legs as if he meant them not
to leave the ground but they did, just enough, just a
little sideways just enough, and that was all. He lived a

long time doing nothing but that and he is still living just living enough.

The next dog and this is important because it is the next dog. His name is Never Sleeps although he sleeps enough.

He was brown not a dark brown but a light brown and he had a lot of friends who always went about together and they all had to be brown, otherwise Never Sleeps would not let them come along. But all that was later, first he had to be born.

It was not so easy to be born.

There was a dog who was an Alsatian wolf-hound a very nice one, and they knew that in the zoo there was a real wolf quite a nice one. So one night they took the dog to see the wolf and they left her there all night. She liked the wolf and the wolf was lonesome and they stayed together and then later she had a little dog and he was a very nice one, and her name was Never Sleeps. She was a gentle dog and liked to lie in the water in the winter and to be quiet in the summer. She never was a bother.

She could be a mother. She met a white poodle he was still young and he had never had a puppy life because he had not been well. His name was Basket and he looked like one. He was taken to visit Never Sleeps and they were told to be happy together. Never Sleeps was told to play with Basket and teach him how to play. Never Sleeps began, she had to teach catch if you can or tag, and she had to teach him pussy wants a corner and she taught him each one of them.

She taught him tag and even after he played it and much later on when he was dead another Basket he looked just like him went on playing tag. To play tag you have to be able to run forward and back to run around things and to start one way and to go the other way and another dog who is smaller and not so quick has to know how to wait at a corner and go around the other way to make the distance shorter. And sometimes just to see how well tag can be played the bigger quicker dog can even stop to play with a stick or a bone and still get away and not be tagged. That is what it means to play tag and Never Sleeps taught Basket how to play. Then he taught him how to play pussy wants a corner, to play this there have to be trees. Dogs cannot play this in the house they are not allowed to and so they have to have at least four trees if there are three dogs and three trees if there are two dogs to play pussy wants a corner. Never Sleeps preferred tag to pussy wants a corner but Basket rather liked best pussy wants a corner.

Ida never knew who knew what she said, she never knew what she said because she listened and as she listened well the moon scarcely the moon but still there is a moon.

Very likely hers was the moon.

Ida knew she never had been a little sister or even a little brother. Ida knew.

So scarcely was there an absence when some one died.

Believe it or not some one died.

And he was somebody's son and Ida began to cry and he was twenty-six and Ida began to cry and Ida was not alone and she began to cry.

Ida had never cried before, but now she began to cry.

Even when Andrew came back from his walk and talked about his walk, Ida began to cry.

It's funny about crying. Ida knew it was funny about crying, she listened at the radio and they played the national anthem and Ida began to cry. It is funny about crying.

But anyway Ida was sitting and she was there and one by one somebody said Thank you, have you heard of me. And she always had. That was Ida.

Even Andrew had he had heard of them, that was the way he had been led to be ready to take his walk every day because he had heard of every one who came in one after the other one.

And Ida did not cry again.

One day, she saw a star it was an uncommonly large one and when it set it made a cross, she looked and looked and she and did not hear Andrew take a walk and that was natural enough she was not there. They had lost her. Ida was gone.

So she sat up and went to bed carefully and she easily told every one that there was more wind in Texas than in San Francisco and nobody believed her. So she said wait and see and they waited.

She came back to life exactly day before yesterday. And now listen.

Ida loved three men. One was an officer who was not killed but he might have been, one was a painter who was not in hospital but he might have been one and one was a lawyer who had gone away to Montana and she had never heard from him.

Ida loved each one of them and went to say good-bye to them.

Good-bye, good-bye she said, and she did say good-bye to them.

She wondered if they were there, of course she did not go away. What she really wanted was Andrew, where oh where was Andrew.

Andrew was difficult to suit and so Ida did not suit him. But Ida did sit down beside him.

Ida fell in love with a young man who had an adventure. He came from Kansas City and he knew that he was through. He was twenty years old. His uncle had died of meningitis, so had his father and so had his cousin, his name was Mark and he had a mother but no sisters and he had a wife and sisters-in-law.

Ida looked the other way when they met, she knew Mark would die when he was twenty-six and he did but before that he had said, For them, they like me for them and Ida had answered just as you say Mark. Ida always bent her head when she saw Mark she was tall and she bent her head when she saw Mark, he was tall and broad and Ida bent her head when she saw him. She knew he would die of meningitis and he did. That was why Ida always bent her head when she saw him.

Why should everybody talk about Ida.

Why not.

Dear Ida.

PART TWO

IDA WAS almost married to Andrew and not anybody
could cloud it. It was very important that she was almost
married to Andrew. Besides he was Andrew the first. All
the others had been others.

Nobody talked about the color of Ida's hair and they
talked about her a lot, nor the color of her eyes.

She was sitting and she dreamed that Andrew was a
soldier. She dreamed well not dreamed but just dreamed.
The day had been set for their marriage and everything
had been ordered. Ida was always careful about order-
ing, food clothes cars, clothes food cars everything was
well chosen and the day was set and then the telephone
rang and it said that Andrew was dying, he had not been
killed he was only dying, and Ida knew that the food
would do for the people who came to the funeral and the
car would do to go to the funeral and the clothes would
not do dear me no they would not do and all of this was
just dreaming. Ida was alive yet and so was Andrew, she

had been sitting, he had been walking and he came home and told about his walk and Ida was awake and she was listening and Andrew was Andrew the first, and Ida was Ida and they were almost married and not anybody could cloud anything.

P A R T T H R E E

ANY BALL has to look like the moon. Ida just had to know what was going to be happening soon.

They can be young so young they can go in swimming. Ida had been. Not really swimming one was learning and the other was teaching.

This was being young in San Francisco and the baths were called Lurline Baths. Ida was young and so was he they were both good both she and he and he was teaching her how to swim, he leaned over and he said kick he was holding her under the chin and he was standing beside her, it was not deep water, and he said kick and she did and he walked along beside her holding her chin, and he said kick and she kicked again and he was standing very close to her and she kicked hard and she kicked him. He let go her he called out Jesus Christ my balls and he went under and she went under, they were neither of them drowned but they might have been.

Strangely enough she never thought about Frank, that

was his name, Frank, she could not remember his other
name, but once when she smelled wild onion she remembered going under and that neither were drowned.

It is difficult never to have been younger but Ida almost was she almost never had been younger.

PART FOUR

AND NOW it was suddenly happening, well not suddenly but it was happening, Andrew was almost Andrew the first. It was not sudden.

They always knew what he could do, that is not what he would do but what they had to do to him. Ida knew.

Andrew the first, walked every day and came back to say where he had walked that day. Every day he walked the same day and every day he told Ida where he had walked that day. Yes Ida.

Ida was just as much older as she had been.

Yes Ida.

One day Ida was alone. When she was alone she was lying down and when she was not alone she was lying down. Everybody knew everything about Ida, everybody did. They knew that when she was alone she was lying down and when she was not alone she was lying down.

Everybody knew everything about Ida and by everybody, everybody means everybody.

It might have been exciting that everybody knew

everything about Ida and it did not excite Ida it soothed Ida. She was soothed.

For a four.

She shut the door.

They dropped in.

And drank gin.

I'd like a conversation said Ida.

So one of them told that when his brother was a soldier, it was in summer and he ate an apple off an apple tree a better apple than he had ever eaten before, so he took a slip of the tree and he brought it home and after he put it into the ground where he was and when he took it home he planted it and now every year they had apples off this apple tree.

Another one told how when his cousin was a soldier, he saw a shepherd dog, different from any shepherd dog he had ever seen and as he knew a man who kept sheep, he took the shepherd dog home with him and gave it to the man and now all the shepherd dogs came from the dog his cousin had brought home with him from the war.

Another one was telling that a friend of his had a sister-in-law and the sister-in-law had the smallest and the finest little brown dog he had ever seen, and he asked the sister-in-law what race it was and where she had gotten it. Oh she said a soldier gave it to me for my little girl, he had brought it home with him and he gave it to my little girl and she and he play together, they always play together.

Ida listened to them and she sighed, she was resting, and she said, I like lilies-of-the-valley too do you, and they all said they did, and one of them said, when his sister had been a nurse in a war she always gathered lilies-of-the-valley before they were in flower. Oh yes said Ida.

And so there was a little conversation and they all said they would stay all evening. They said it was never dark when they stayed all evening and Ida sighed and said yes she was resting.

Once upon a time Ida took a train, she did not like trains, and she never took them but once upon a time she took a train. They were fortunate, the train went on running and Andrew was not there. Then it stopped and Ida got out and Andrew still was not there. He was not expected but still he was not there. So Ida went to eat something.

This did happen to Ida.

They asked what she would have to eat and she said she would eat the first and the last that they had and not anything in between. Andrew always ate everything but Ida when she was alone she ate the first and the last of everything, she was not often alone so it was not often that she could eat the first and the last of everything but she did that time and then everybody helped her to leave but not not to get on a train again.

She never did get on any train again. Naturally not, she was always there or she was resting. Her life had

every minute when it was either this or that and sometimes both, either she was there or she was resting and
sometimes it was both.

Her life never began again because it was always there.

And now it was astonishing that it was always there.
Yes it was.

Ida

Yes it was.

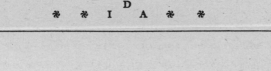

PART FIVE

ANY FRIEND of Ida's could be run over by any little thing.

Not Andrew, Andrew was Andrew the first and regular.

Why are sailors, farmers and actors more given to reading and believing signs than other people. It is natural enough for farmers and sailors who are always there where signs are, alone with them but why actors.

Well anyway Ida was not an actress nor a sailor nor a farmer.

Cuckoos magpies crows and swallows are signs.

Nightingales larks robins and orioles are not.

Ida saw her first glow worm. The first of anything is a sign.

Then she saw three of them that was a sign.

Then she saw ten.

Ten are never a sign.

And yet what had she caught.

She had caught and she had taught.

That ten was not a sign.

Andrew was Andrew the first.

He was a sign.

Ida had not known he was a sign, not known he was a sign.

Ida was resting.

Worse than any signs is a family who brings bad luck. Ida had known one, naturally it was a family of women, a family which brings bad luck must be all women.

Ida had known one the kind that if you take a dog with you when you go to see them, the dog goes funny and when it has its puppies its puppies are peculiar.

This family was a mother a daughter and a grand-daughter, well they all had the airs and graces of beauties and with reason, well they were. The grandmother had been married to an admiral and then he died and to a general and then he died. Her daughter was married to a doctor but the doctor could not die, he just left, the granddaughter was very young, just as young as six-teen, she married a writer, nobody knows just how not but before very long she cried, every day she cried, and her mother cried and even her grandmother and then she was not married any longer to the writer. Then well she was still young not yet twenty-one and a banker saw her and he said he must marry her, well she couldn't yet naturally not the writer was still her husband but very soon he would not be, so the banker was all but married to her, well anyway they went out together, the car turned over the banker was dead and she had broken her collar-bone.

Now everybody wanted to know would the men want her more because of all this or would they be scared of her.

Well as it happened it was neither the one nor the other. It often is not.

The men after that just did not pay any attention to her. You might say they did not any of them pay any attention to her even when she was twenty-three or twenty-four. They did not even ask not any of them. What for.

And so anybody could see that they could not bring good luck to any one not even a dog, no not even.

No really bad luck came to Ida from knowing them but after that anyway, it did happen that she never went out to see any one.

She said it was better.

She did not say it was better but it was better. Ida never said anything about anything.

Anyway after that she rested and let them come in, anybody come in. That way no family would come that just would not happen.

So Ida was resting and they came in. Not one by one, they just came in.

That is the way Andrew came he just came in.

He took a walk every afternoon and he always told about what happened on his walk.

He just walked every afternoon.

He liked to hear people tell about good luck and bad luck.

Somebody one afternoon told a whole lot.

Andrew was like that, he was born with his life, why not. And he had it, he walked every afternoon, and he said something every minute of every day, but he did not talk while he was listening. He listened while he was listening but he did not hear unless he asked to have told what they were telling. He liked to hear about good luck and bad luck because it was not real to him, nothing was real to him except a walk every afternoon and to say something every minute of every day.

So he said, and what were you saying about good luck and bad luck.

Well it was this.

The things anybody has to worry about are spiders, cuckoos goldfish and dwarfs.

Yes said Andrew. And he was listening.

Spider at night makes delight.

Spider in the morning makes mourning.

Yes said Andrew.

Well, said the man who was talking, think of a spider talking.

Yes said Andrew.

The spider says

Listen to me I, I am a spider, you must not mistake me for the sky, the sky red at night is a sailor's delight, the sky red in the morning is a sailor's warning, you must not mistake me for the sky, I am I, I am a spider and in the morning any morning I bring sadness and mourning and at night if they see me at night I bring them delight, do not mistake me for the sky, not I, do not mistake me for a dog who howls at night and causes no delight, a dog says the bright moonlight makes him go mad with desire to bring sorrow to any one sorrow and sadness, the dog says the night the bright moonlight brings madness and grief, but says the spider I, I am a spider, a big spider or a little spider, it is all alike, a spider green or gray, there is nothing else to say, I am a spider and I know and I always tell everybody so, to see me at night brings them delight, to see me in the morning, brings mourning, and if you see me at night, and I am a sight, because I am dead having died up by night, even so dead at night I still cause delight, I dead bring delight to any one who sees me at night, and so every one can sleep tight who has seen me at night.

Andrew was listening and he said it was interesting and said did they know any other superstition.

Yes said the man there is the cuckoo.

Oh yes the cuckoo.

Supposing they could listen to a cuckoo.

I, I am a cuckoo, I am not a clock, because a clock makes time pass and I stop the time by giving mine, and mine is money, and money is honey, and I I bring money, I, I, I. I bring misery and money but never honey, listen to me.

Once I was there, you know everybody, that I I sing in the spring, sweetly, sing, evening and morning and everything.

Listen to me.

If you listen to me, if when you hear me, the first time in the spring time, hear me sing, and you have money a lot of money for you in your pocket when you hear me in the spring, you will be rich all year any year, but if you hear me and you have gone out with no money jingling in your pocket when you hear me singing then you will be poor poor all year, poor.

But sometimes I can do even more.

I knew a case like that, said the man.

Did you said Andrew.

She, well she, she had written a lovely book but nobody took the lovely book nobody paid her money for the lovely book they never gave her money, never never never and she was poor and they needed money oh yes they did she and her lover.

And she sat and she wrote and she longed for money for she had a lover and all she needed was money to live and love, money money money.

So she wrote and she hoped and she wrote and she sighed and she wanted money, money money, for herself and for love for love and for herself, money money money.

And one day somebody was sorry for her and they gave her not much but a little money, he was a nice millionaire the one who gave her a little money, but it was very little money and it was spring and she wanted love and money and she had love and now she wanted money.

She went out it was the spring and she sat upon the grass with a little money in her pocket and the cuckoo saw her sitting and knew she had a little money and it went up to her close up to her and sat on a tree and said cuckoo at her, cuckoo cuckoo, cuckoo, and she said, Oh, a cuckoo bird is singing on a cuckoo tree singing to me oh singing to me. And the cuckoo sang cuckoo cuckoo and she sang cuckoo cuckoo to it, and there they were singing cuckoo she to it and it to her.

Then she knew that it was true and that she would be rich and love would not leave her and she would have all three money and love and a cuckoo in a tree, all three.

Andrew did listen and the man went on.

And the goldfish.

Yes said a goldfish I listen I listen but listen to me I am stronger than a cuckoo stronger and meaner because I never do bring good luck I bring nothing but misery and trouble and all no not at all I bring no good luck only bad and that does not make me sad it makes me glad that I never bring good luck only bad.

They buy me because I look so pretty and red and gold in my bowl but I never bring good luck I only bring bad, bad bad bad.

Listen to me.

There was a painter once who thought he was so big he could do anything and he did. So he bought goldfish and any day he made a painting of us in the way that made him famous and made him say, goldfish bring me good luck not bad, and they better had.

Everything went wonderfully for him, he turned goldfish into gold because everything he did was bold and it sold, and he had money and fame but all the same we the goldfish just sat and waited while he painted.

One day, crack, the bowl where we were fell apart and we were all cracked the bowl the water and the fish, and the painter too crack went the painter and his painting too and he woke up and he knew that he was dead too, the goldfish and he, they were all dead, but we there are always goldfish in plenty to bring bad luck to anybody too but he the painter and his painting was dead dead dead.

We knew what to do.

Andrew was more interested, and the dwarfs he said.

Well this is the way they are they say we are two male and female, if you see us both at once it means nothing, but if you see either of us alone it means bad luck or good. And which is which. Misfortune is female good luck luck is male, it is all very simple.

Oh yes anybody can know that and if they see one of us and it is the female he or she has to go and go all day long until they see a dwarf man, otherwise anything awful could happen to them. A great many make fun of those who believe in this thing but those who believe they know, female dwarf bad luck male dwarf good luck, all that is eternal.

Silence.

Suddenly the goldfish suddenly began to swish and to bubble and squeak and to shriek, I I do not believe in dwarfs neither female nor male, he cried, no not in a cuckoo, no not in spiders, no, the only thing I believe in besides myself is a shoe on a table, oh that, that makes me shiver and shake, I have no shoes no feet no shoes but a shoe on a table, that is terrible, oh oh yes oh ah.

And the cuckoo said,

Oh you poor fish, you do not believe in me, you poor fish, and I do not believe in you fish nothing but fish a goldfish only fish, no I do not believe in you no fish no, I believe in me, I am a cuckoo and I know and I tell you so, no the only thing I believe in which is not me is when I see the new moon through a glass window, I never do because there is no glass to see through, but I believe in that too, I believe in that and I believe in me ah yes I do I see what I see through, and I do I do I do.

No I do not believe in a fish, nor in a dwarf nor in a spider not I, because I am I a cuckoo and I, I, I.

The spider screamed. You do not believe in me, everybody believes in me, you do not believe in spiders you do not believe in me bah. I believe in me I am all there is to see except well if you put your clothes on wrong side to well that is an awful thing to do, and if you change well that is worse than any way and what do I say, if you put your clothes on wrong everything will go well that day but if you change from wrong to right then nothing will

go right, but what can I do I am a green spider or a gray
and I have the same clothes every day and I can make no
mistake any day but I believe oh I believe if you put your
clothes on wrong side to everything will be lovely that you
do, but anyway everybody has to believe in me, a spider,
of course they do, a spider in the morning is an awful
warning a spider at night brings delight, it is so lovely
to know this is true and not to believe in a fish or in dwarfs
or in a cuckoo, ooh ooh, it is I, no matter what they try
it is I I. I.

The dwarfs said, And of whom are you talking all of
you, we dwarfs, we are in the beginning we have commenced everything and we believe in everything yes we
do, we believe in the language of flowers and we believe
in lucky stones, we believe in peacocks' feathers and we
believe in stars too, we believe in leaves of tea, we believe
in a white horse and a red-headed girl, we believe in the
moon, we believe in red in the sky, we believe in the bark-
ing of a dog, we believe in everything that is mortal and
immortal, we even believe in spiders, in goldfish and in
the cuckoo, we the dwarfs we believe in it all, all and all,
and all and every one are alike, we are, all the world is
like us the dwarfs, all the world believes in everything
and we do too and all the world believes in us and in you.

Everybody in the room was quiet and Andrew was
really excited and he looked at Ida and that was that.

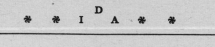
P A R T   S I X

GOOD LUCK and bad luck.

No luck and then luck.

Ida was resting.

She was nearly Ida was ready nearly well.

She could tell when she had been settled when she had been settled very well.

Once she had been and she liked it, she liked to be in one room and to have him in another room and to talk across to him while she was resting. Then she had been settled very well. It did not settle everything, nothing was unsettling, but she had been settled very well.

Andrew had a mother.

Some still have one and some do not still have one but Andrew did still have a mother.

He had other things beside

But he had never had a bride.

Flowers in the spring succeed each other with extraor-

dinary rapidity and the ones that last the longest if
you do not pick them are the violets.

Andrew had his life, he was never alone and he was
never left and he was never active and he was never quiet
and he was never sad.

He was Andrew.

It came about that he had never gone anywhere unless
he had known beforehand he was going to go there, but
and he had, he had gone to see Ida and once he was there
it was as if he had been going to see Ida. So naturally he
was always there.

Andrew knew that he was the first Andrew.

He had a nervous cough but he was not nervous.

He had a quiet voice but he talked loudly.

He had a regular life but he did what he did as if he
would do it and he always did. Obstinate you call him.
Well if you like. He said obstinate was not a word.

Ida never spoke, she just said what she pleased. Dear
Ida.

It began not little by little, but it did begin.

Who has houses said a friend of Ida's.

Everybody laughed.

But said Andrew I understand when you speak.

Nobody laughed.

It was not customary to laugh.

Three makes more exchange than two.

There were always at least three.

This was a habit with Andrew.

Ida had no habit, she was resting.

And so little by little somebody knew.

How kindly if they do not bow.

Ida had a funny habit. She had once heard that alba-trosses which birds she liked the name of always bowed before they did anything. Ida bowed like this to anything she liked. If she had a hat she liked, she had many hats but sometimes she had a hat she liked and if she liked it she put it on a table and bowed to it. She had many dresses and sometimes she really liked one of them. She would put it somewhere then and then she would bow to it. Of course jewels but really dresses and hats particularly hats, sometimes particularly dresses. Nobody knew any-thing about this certainly not anybody and certainly not Andrew, if anybody knew it would be an accident because when Ida bowed like that to a hat or a dress she never said it. A maid might come to know but naturally never hav-ing heard about albatrosses, the maid would not under-stand.

Oh yes said Ida while she was resting. Naturally she never bowed while she was resting and she was always resting when they were there.

Dear Ida.

It came to be that any day was like Saturday to Ida.

And slowly it came to be that even to Andrew any day came to be Saturday. Saturday had never been especially a day to Andrew but slowly it came to be Saturday and then every day began to be Saturday as it had come to be to Ida.

Of course there was once a song, every day will be Sunday by and by.

Ida knew this about Saturday, she always had, and now Andrew slowly came to know it too. Of course he did walk every day walk even if every day was Saturday. You can't change everything even if everything is changed.

Anybody could begin to realize what life was to Andrew what life had been to Andrew what life was going to be to Andrew.

Andrew was remarkable insofar as it was all true. Yes indeed it was.

Saturday, Ida.

Ida never said once upon a time. These words did not mean anything to Ida. This is what Ida said. Ida said yes, and then Ida said oh yes, and then Ida said, I said yes, and then Ida said, Yes.

Once when Ida was excited she said I know what it is I do, I do know that it is, yes.

That is what she said when she was excited.

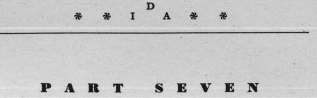

PART SEVEN

ANDREW KNEW that nobody would be so rude as not to remember Andrew. And this was true. They did remember him. Until now. Now they do not remember Andrew. But Andrew knew that nobody would be so rude as not to. And pretty well it was true.

But again.

Andrew never had to think. He never had to say that it was a pleasant day. But it was always either wet or dry or cold or warm or showery or just going to be. All that was enough for Andrew and Ida never knew whether there was any weather. That is the reason they got on so well together.

There was never any beginning or end, but every day came before or after another day. Every day did.

Little by little circles were open and when they were open they were always closed.

This was just the way it was.

Supposing Ida was at home, she was almost at home and when she was at home she was resting.

Andrew had many things to do but then it was always true that he was with Ida almost all day although he never came to stay and besides she was resting.

One of the things Ida never liked was a door.

People should be there and not come through a door.

As much as possible Ida did not let herself know that, they did come through a door.

She did not like to go out to dinner at a house because you had to come in through a door. A restaurant was different there is really no door. She liked a room well enough but she did not like a door.

Andrew was different, he did just naturally come through a door, he came through a door, he was the first to come through a doorway and the last to come through a doorway. Doorways and doors were natural to him. He and Ida never talked about this, you might say they never talked about anything certainly they never talked about doors.

The French say a door has to be open or shut but open or shut did not interest Ida what she really minded was that there was a door at all. She did not really mind standing in a portiere or in a hall, but she did not like doors. Of course it was natural enough feeling as she did about doors that she never went out to see anybody. She went out she liked to go out but not through a doorway. There it was that was the way she was.

One day she was telling about this, she said, if you stand in an open place in a house and talk to somebody who can hear that is very nice, if you are out or in it is very nice but doors doors are never nice.

She did not remember always being that way about doors, she kind of did not remember doors at all, it was not often she mentioned doors, but she just did not care about doors.

One day did not come after another day to Ida. Ida never took on yesterday or tomorrow, she did not take on months either nor did she take on years. Why should she when she had always been the same, what ever happened there she was, no doors and resting and everything happening. Sometimes something did happen, she knew to whom she had been married but that was not anything happening, she knew about clothes and resting but that was not anything happening. Really there really was never anything happening although everybody knew everything was happening.

It was dark in winter and light in summer but that did not make any difference to Ida. If somebody said to her you know they are most awfully kind, Ida could always say I know I do not like that kind. She liked to be pleasant and she was but kind, well yes she knew that kind.

They asked her to a dinner party but she did not go, her husband went, she had a husband then and he wore a wedding ring. Husbands do not often wear wedding rings but he did. Ida knew when he came home that he had worn his wedding ring, she said, not very well and he said oh yes very well.

Three things had happened to Ida and they were far away but not really because she liked to rest and be there. She always was.

Andrew next to that was nothing and everything, Andrew knew a great many people who were very kind. Kind people always like doors and doorways, Andrew did. Andrew thought about Ida and doors, why should he when doors were there. But for Ida doors were not there if they had been she would not have been. How can you rest if there are doors. And resting is a pleasant thing.

So life went on little by little for Ida and Andrew.

It all did seem just the same but all the same it was not just the same. How could anybody know, nobody could know but there it was. Well no there it wasn't.

Ida began talking.

She never began but sometimes she was talking, she did not understand so she said, she did not sit down so she said, she did not stand up so she said, she did not go out or come in, so she said. And it was all true enough.

This was Ida

Dear Ida.

Ida was good friends with all her husbands, she was always good friends with all her husbands.

She always remembered that the first real hat she ever had was a turban made of pansies. The second real hat she ever had was a turban made of poppies.

For which she was interested in pansies and gradually she was not. She had liked pansies and heliotrope, then she liked wild flowers, then she liked tube-roses, then she liked orchids and then she was not interested in flowers.

Of course she was not interested. Flowers should stay where they grow, there was no door for flowers to come through, they should stay where they grew. She was more interested in birds than in flowers but she was not really interested in birds.

Anything that was given to her she thanked for she liked to thank, some people do not but she did and she liked to be thanked. Yes she said.

She was careful to sit still when she thanked or was thanked, it is better so.

Some people like to stand or to move when they thank or are thanked but not Ida, she was not really resting when she thanked or was thanked but she was sitting.

Nobody knew what Ida was going to do although she always did the same thing in the same way, but still nobody knew what Ida was going to do or what she was going to say. She said yes. That is what Ida did say.

Everybody knew that they would not forget Andrew but was it true.

Not so sure.

You did not have to be sure about any such thing as long as it was happening, which it was not.

Andrew come in said Ida.

Andrew was in.

Andrew do not come in said Ida. Ida said Andrew is not coming in. Andrew came in.

Andrew had not been brought up to come in but little
by little he did come in he came in and when Ida said he
is not to come in he came in. This was natural as he came
to know Ida. Anybody came in who came to know Ida but
Ida did not say come in. To Andrew she had said yes
come in and Andrew had come in.

It was not a natural life for Andrew this life of coming in and this was what had been happening to Andrew,
he had commenced to come in and then he never did anything else, he always came in. He should have been doing
something else but he did not he just came in.

Little by little it happened that except that he took
his walk in the afternoon he never did anything but
come in. This little by little was everything Andrew did.

She tried to stop, not anything but she tried to stop
but how could she stop if she was resting how could she
stop Andrew from coming in.

And in this way it might happen to come to be true
that anybody would forget Andrew.

That would not happen little by little but it could
come to be true.

Even in a book they could be rude and forget Andrew
but not now. Andrew said not now, and Ida said Andrew
said not now and Ida said she said not now but really
Ida did not say not now she just said no.

Ida often sighed not very often but she did sigh and
when somebody came in she said yes I always say yes,

if you say no then you say no but if you say yes then you just say yes.

This was very natural and Ida was very natural.

So much happened but nothing happened to Ida.

To have anything happen you have to choose and Ida never chose, how could she choose, you can choose hats and you can choose other things but that is not choosing. To choose, well to choose, Ida never chose. And then it looked as if it happened, and it did happen and it was happening and it went on happening. How excited, and Ida was excited and so was Andrew and his name might have been William.

He had a great many names Andrew did and one of them was William but when he became Andrew the first he could not be William.

Ida often wished gently that he had been William, it is easier to say William than Andrew and Ida had naturally to say a name. Every time Andrew came in or was there or was anywhere she had to say his name and if his name had been William she could have said it easier. But all the same it was easy enough to say Andrew and she said Andrew.

Sometimes she called him Andy and sometimes she would say Handy Andy it is handy to have Andy, and her saying that did please Andrew. Naturally enough it pleased him.

It is not easy to lead a different life, much of it never happens but when it does it is different.

So Ida and Andrew never knew but it was true they were to lead a different life and yet again they were not.

If one did the other did not, and if the other did then the other did not.

And this is what happened.

If they had any friends they had so many friends.

They were always accompanied, Andrew when he came and went and wherever he was, Ida was not accompanied but she was never alone and when they were together they were always accompanied.

This was natural enough because Andrew always had been and it was natural enough because Ida always had been.

Men were with them and women were with them and men and women were with them.

It was this that made Ida say let's talk.

It was this that made Ida say, I like to know that all I love to do is to say something and he hears me.

It was this that made Ida say I never could though they were not glad to come.

It was this that made Ida say how do you do do come. It was this that made Ida say yes everything I can do I can always ask Andrew and Andrew will always do anything I ask him to do and that is the reason I call him Handy Andy.

Ida never laughed she smiled and sometimes she yawned and sometimes she closed her eyes and sometimes she opened them and she rested. That is what Ida did.

It did look as if nothing could change, nothing could change Ida that was true, and if that was true could anything change Andrew.

In a way nothing could but he could come not to be Andrew and if he were not Andrew Ida would not call him Handy Andy and as a matter of fact when he was not any longer Andrew she never did call him Handy Andy. She called him Andy, and she called him Andrew then but that was not the same thing.

But it was natural enough. Nature is not natural and that is natural enough.

Ida knew that is she did not exactly know then but all the same she did know then some people who always were ready to be there.

The larger the house these people had the more ready they were to be there.

Ida might have come to that but if she did she could not rest.

Oh dear she often said oh dear isn't it queer.

More than that she needed no help, but she might come to need help, and if she would come to need help she would help herself and if she helped herself then she certainly would be needing help.

I let it alone, she told everybody, and she did. She certainly did. But most gradually Andrew it was true was a way to do, not for Ida, but for Andrew, and that made a lot of trouble, not for Ida, but for Andrew.

What was because was just what was a bother to Ida

because she saw that Andrew was across from where he was.

Nobody knew whether it was happening slowly or not. It might be slowly and it might not.

Once in a great while Ida got up suddenly.

When she did well it was sudden, and she went away not far away but she left. That happened once in a way. She was sitting just sitting, they said if you look out of the window you see the sun. Oh yes said Ida, and they said, do you like sunshine or rain and Ida said she liked it best. She was sitting of course and she was resting and she did like it best.

They said, well anybody said, More than enough. Oh yes said Ida, I like it, yes I do, I like it.

Somebody said, well let us go on. No said Ida I always say no, no said Ida. And why not they asked her, well said Ida if you go away. We did not say we were going away, they said. Believe it or not we did not say we were going away, they said. Well said Ida I feel that way too. Do you they said. Yes said Ida I feel that way too.

It was not then that she got up suddenly. It was considerably after. She was not startled, a dog might bark suddenly but she was not startled. She was never startled at once. If she was, well she never was.

But after all, if she got up suddenly, and she did not very often. And once she got up suddenly, she left.

That did not as a matter of fact make very much difference.

More than enough she never really said, but once well really once she did get up suddenly and if she did get up suddenly she went away.

Nobody ever heard Andrew ever mention what he did because he never did it.

Everybody always said something, they said let's have it again, and they always had it again.

For this much they did come in, of course there never really was a beginning, for which it was fortunate.

Ida was mostly fortunate even if it did not matter. It really did not matter, not much.

So whether it was slowly or not was not enough because nobody was scared. They might be careful Ida was careful.

For which reason she was never worried not very likely to be.

She once said when this you see remember me, she liked being like that. Nicely.

For this reason she was rested. She will get up suddenly once and leave but not just now. Not now.

They could exchange well she knew more about hats than cows.

Andrew was interested in cows and horses. But after all there was much more in the way they sat down. Believe it or not they did sit down.

PART EIGHT

WELL HE SAID Andrew said that he could not do without Ida. Ida said yes, and indeed when she said yes she meant yes. Yes Andrew could not do without Ida and Ida said yes. She knew she might go away suddenly, but she said yes.

And so it came to be not more exciting but more yes than it had been.

Ida did say yes.

And Andrew was not nervous that is to say Andrew trembled easily but he was not nervous. Ida was nervous and so she said yes. If you are resting and you say yes you can be nervous, and Ida was nervous. There was no mistake about Ida's being nervous. She was not nervous again, she was just nervous. When she said yes she was not nervous. When she was resting she was nervous. Nearly as well as ever she said she was, she said she was nearly as well as ever, but nobody ever asked her if she is well, they always knew she was nearly as well as ever.

It happened that when she went out she came in. Well she did go out and when she went out she came in.

Anyhow went in and went out, but Ida did not.

When she went out she came in.

This was not just in the beginning it came to be more so, the only time that it ever was otherwise was when she got up suddenly and this did happen soon.

And so Andrew well Andrew was not careless nothing ever made Andrew careless.

He was much prepared.

Neither Andrew nor Ida was astonished but they were surprised. They had that in common that they were surprised not suddenly surprised but just surprised.

They were not astonished to learn but they were surprised.

This is what happened.

Ida had an aunt, she remembered she had an aunt but that had nothing to do with Ida nothing at all. Next to nothing to do with Ida.

Her aunt well her aunt sometimes did not feel that way about it but not very often and really it had nothing to do with Ida or with what happened.

What happened was this.

Ida returned more and more to be Ida. She even said she was Ida.

What, they said. Yes, she said. And they said why do you say yes. Well she said I say yes because I am Ida.

It got quite exciting. It was not just exciting it was

D

quite exciting. Every time she said yes, and she said yes any time she said anything, well any time she said yes it was quite exciting.

Ida even was excited, well not altogether but she really was excited. Even Andrew was excited and as for the rest of all of them, all of them were excited.

And in between, well Ida always did have a tendency to say yes and now she did say, she even sometimes said oh yes.

Everybody was excited, it was extraordinary the way everybody was excited, they were so excited that everybody stopped everything to be excited.

Ida was excited but not very excited. At times she was not excited but she did always say yes.

Andrew was excited, he was not excited when he took his walk but he was quite often excited. Ida did say yes.

They went out together of course but it was difficult as the more excited he was the faster he went and the more excited she was the slower she went and as she could not go faster and he could not go slower. Well it was all right.

They lived from day to day. Ida did. So did they all. Some of their friends used to look at clouds, they would come in and say this evening I saw a cloud and it looked like a hunting dog and others would say he saw a cloud that looked like a dragon, and another one would say he said a cloud that looked like a dream, and another he saw a cloud that looked like a queen. Ida said yes and Andrew said very nicely. They liked people to come in and tell what kind of clouds they had seen. Some had seen a cloud that looked like a fish and some had seen a cloud that looked like a rhinoceros, almost any of them had seen a cloud.

It was very pleasant for Ida that they came and told what the clouds they had seen looked like.

Ida lived from day to day so did they all but all the same a day well a day was not really all day to Ida, she needed only a part of the day and only a part of the night, the rest of the day and night she did not need. They might but she did not.

Andrew did not need day nor night but he used it all he did not use it up but he used it, he used it all of it it was necessary to use all of it and it was always arranged that he did everything that was necessary to do and he did. It was necessary that he used all of the night and all of the day every day and every night. This was right.

Ida chose just that piece of the day and just that piece of the night that she would use.

All right.

They did not say it but she said it and that was why she said yes.

And then something did happen.

What happened was this.

Everybody began to miss something and it was not a kiss, you bet your life it was not a kiss that anybody began to miss. And yet perhaps it was.

Well anyway something did happen and it excited every one that it was something and that it did happen.

It happened slowly and then it was happening and then it happened a little quicker and then it was happening and then it happened it really happened and then it had happened and then it was happening and then well then there it was and if it was there then it is there only now nobody can care.

And all this sounds kind of funny but it is all true.

And it all began with everybody knowing that they were missing something and perhaps a kiss but not really nobody really did miss a kiss. Certainly not Ida.

Ida was not interested, she was resting and then it began oh so slowly to happen and then there it was all right there it was everybody knew it all right there it was.

Dear Ida.

What happened.

Well what happened was this. Everybody thought everybody knew what happened. And everybody did know and so it was that that happened. Nothing was neglected that is Ida did nothing Andrew did nothing but nothing was neglected.

When something happens nothing begins. When anything begins then nothing happens and you could always say with Ida that nothing began.

Nothing ever did begin.

Partly that and partly nothing more. And there was never any need of excuses. You only excuse yourself if you begin or if somebody else begins but with Ida well she never began and nobody else began. Andrew although he was different was the same, he was restless all day and Ida was resting all day but neither one nor the other had to begin. So in a way nothing did happen.

That was the way it was nothing did happen everybody talked all day and every day about Ida and Andrew but nothing could happen as neither the one of them or the other one ever did begin anything.

It is wonderful how things pile up even if nothing is added. Very wonderful.

Suppose somebody comes in, suppose they say, well how are we today. Well supposing they do say that. It does not make any difference but supposing they do say that. Somebody else comes in and says that too well how are we today. Well if Ida had not answered the first one she could not answer the second one because you always have to answer the first one before you answer the second one.

And if there was still a third one and mostly there was and a fourth one and a fifth one and even a sixth one and each one said well and how are we today, it is natural enough that Ida would have nothing to say. She had not answered the first one and if you are resting you cannot hurry enough to catch up and so she had nothing to say. Yes she said. It is natural enough that she said yes, because she did not catch up with anything and did not interrupt anything and did not begin anything and did not stop anything.

Yes said Ida.

It looks the same but well of course one can run away, even if you are resting you can run away. Not necessarily but you can. You can run away even if you say yes. And if you run away well you never come back even if you are completely followed.

This could be a thing that Ida would do. She would say yes and she was resting and nothing happened and nothing began but she could run away. Not everybody can but she could and she did.

What happened.

Before she ran away.

She did not really run away, she did not go away. It was something in between. She took her umbrella and parasol. Everybody knew she was going, that is not really true they did not know she was going but she went, they knew she was going. Everybody knew.

She went away that is she did get away and when she was away everybody was excited naturally enough. It was better so. Dear Ida.

Little by little she was not there she was elsewhere. Little by little.

It was little by little and it was all of a sudden. It was not entirely sudden because she was not entirely there before she was elsewhere.

That is the way it happened.

Before it happened well quite a while before it happened she did meet women. When they came she was resting, when they went she was resting, she liked it and they did not mind it. They came again and when they came again, she was obliging, she did say yes. She was sorry she was resting, so sorry and she did say yes. She thought they liked it and they did but it was not the same as if she had ever said no or if she had not always been resting.

If she had not always been resting they would not have come nor would they have come again. They said thank you my dear when they went. She had said yes Ida had and she said yes again.

That is the way it was before going away, they had not really come nor had they said Thank you my dear.

That is really the reason that Ida ran away not ran away or went away but something in between. She was ready to be resting and she was ready to say yes and she was ready to hear them say thank you my dear but they had almost not come again.

So Ida was not there. Dear Ida.

She knew she would be away but not really away but before she knew she was there where she had gone to she was really away.

That was almost an astonishment, quite to her, but to all the others not so much so once she was not there.

Of course she had luncheon and dinners to eat on the way.

One of the menus she ate was this.

She ate soft-shell crabs, she had two servings of soft-shell crabs and she ate lobster à la Newburg she only had one helping of that and then she left.

She often left after she ate. That is when she was not resting but she mostly was resting.

And so there she was and where was Andrew, well Andrew moved quickly while Ida moved slowly that is when they were both nervous, when each one of them was nervous. But he was not there yet. Not really.

Ida was resting. Dear Ida. She said yes.

Slowly little by little Andrew came, Andrew was still his name.

He was just as nervous as he was and he walked every afternoon and then he told about his walk that afternoon. Ida was as nervous as she was and she was resting.

For a little time she did not say yes and then she said yes again.

Gradually it was, well not as it had been but it was, it was quite as it was Ida was resting and she was saying yes but not as much as she had said yes. There were times when she did not say yes times when she was not resting not time enough but times.

It is all very confused but more confused than confusing, and later it was not interesting. It was not confused at all, resting was not confused and yes was not confused but it was interesting.

When any one came well they did Ida could even say how do you do and where did you come from.

Dear Ida.

And if they did not come from anywhere they did not come.

So much for resting.

Little by little there it was. It was Ida and Andrew.

Not too much not too much Ida and not too much Andrew.

And not enough Ida and not enough Andrew.

If Ida goes on, does she go on even when she does not go on any more.

No and yes.

Ida is resting but not resting enough. She is resting but she is not saying yes. Why should she say yes. There is no reason why she should so there is nothing to say.

She sat and when she sat she did not always rest, not enough.

She did rest.

If she said anything she said yes. More than once nothing was said. She said something. If nothing is said then Ida does not say yes. If she goes out she comes in. If she does not go away she is there and she does not go away. She dresses, well perhaps in black why not, and a hat, why not, and another hat, why not, and another dress, why not, so much why not.

She dresses in another hat and she dresses in another dress and Andrew is in, and they go in and that is where they are. They are there. Thank them.

Yes.

GERTRUDE STEIN was born in Pennsylvania in 1874. At Radcliffe she was an outstanding student of William James in psychology, and conducted laboratory experiments with Hugo Munsterberg, which led her to study the anatomy of the brain at Johns Hopkins. In 1902 she joined her brother Leon in Paris, and lived abroad until her death in 1946. Her salon in the rue de Fleurus, over which she presided with Alice B. Toklas, became the gathering place for prominent writers and painters, among them Sherwood Anderson and Hemingway, Matisse and Picasso.